ORIGINS

SHIFTERS FOREVER WORLDS

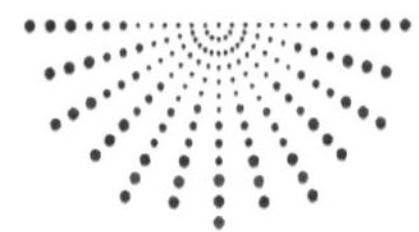

ELLE THORNE

Thank you for reading!

*To receive exclusive updates from Elle Thorne and to be the
first to get your hands on the next release,
please sign up for her newsletter.
Put this in your browser:
ellethorne.com/contact*

ORIGINS

Many millennia ago, a group of Vikings raided a village. As fate would have it, this was the wrong village. It was home of the mighty witch Freyja.

Calder was one of these Vikings. He and his brother lead this band of large, tattooed men with their gruff ways. They've found that one of the villagers' guests has a wealthy husband and can bring a healthy ransom. An amount of silver that will provide great wealth to these Viking fighters.

Brenna can't tell her captors that she won't be able to secure a single piece of silver. Holding her for ransom is pointless. When one of her captors decides that he wants her for a night's pleasure, she's stunned to discover that another saves her. A huge man with tattoos, wielding an ax comes to her defense. Now she's beholden to him.

When Freyja returns to her village to find that the men have been slaughtered and the women and children have been taken prisoners, she renders a punishment that lasts an eternity, and creates two new breeds of beings that will roam the earth in perpetuity.
She also puts Brenna in a difficult decision of choosing love over duty.

Visit www.ElleThorne.com to sign up for Elle's newsletter!

CHAPTER ONE

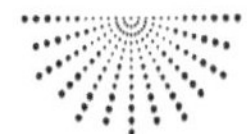

Northlands. Many millennia ago.

The first thing that struck Brenna was the pounding in her head. It hurt so badly, she didn't want to open her eyes. She pressed her fingers against the beating drum that her world had become and was surprised to find a sticky wetness.

That sensation caused her eyes to fly open.

She stared at her fingers as if they'd grown heads.

Blood?

Brenna sat up and surveyed her surroundings. She was in a cell with a thick wooden door and metal bars across the windows.

She rose to her feet slowly. The pounding in her head was joined by dizziness. She reached for the table but miscalculated. She lurched into it, face first, and clipped her temple on the corner, then sent the chair reeling into the table's legs with a crash.

Clutching her forehead, she stayed in the tangle of furs on which she'd been lying.

Furs?

There were no furs like this in her home.

Then—

It came to her; this wasn't home. She was visiting cousins in the north. But this wasn't the guest hut she'd been staying in. No, not at all. The thick door. The bars.

What happened to her head?

"It's about time you woke up, royal one." A male guttural voice came from nearby, one with an accent different than the one she'd grown up with.

She glanced in the direction of the speaker and found a fearsome sight glaring at her from the barred windows in the wooden door.

"Who are you?" she whispered.

"They call me Halvar," he growled. His scowl grew more ferocious. His face had blue paint, or perhaps tattoos, scattered about in patterns that drew attention to his hair, shaved on the sides, long on top and plaited close to his scalp. His brows were drawn, his lips curved down in a sneer. A wild beard hid the bottom half of his face.

"They call me—"

"Oh, we know who you are, my lady. Brenna. The one who will fill our coffers."

A feeling of dread filled her, and she fought to retain her composure. This barbarian had clearly taken her captive. What happened to the rest of the village? To her cousins? To all the others?

"What do you mean?" she dared to ask, though fear threatened to close her throat.

The door rattled; it was being unlocked. Then it swung open.

Halvar appeared even more fierce than before. Furs enhanced his broad shoulders. His arms held more tattoos—intricate designs that spoke of a foreign culture. His eyes were a light blue color, but the irises were ringed with a golden hue.

Then another figure stepped in.

Another man. Just as large, just as fear-inspiring. His face also bearded, but trimmed. His hair, a dirty blond cropped short on the sides, longer on top and was also braided.

The second man's eyes were also blue, but not the light color of Halvar's. His eyes were a dark azure, ringed with the same golden flames. He wore no shirt, and a light blanket of even darker blond hair covered his chest.

But his eyes were different. There was something in them.

He looked directly into her gaze, and for a brief second that seemed to last an eternity, she was captured in that stare, unable to look away, unafraid.

"Halvar," the newcomer said. "Are you frightening

our guest?" He had an accent, just as the first one who had spoken.

At first, his voice was mesmerizing. A deep resonance, entirely male, one that matched his chiseled countenance.

But then it struck her.

Guest?

"If I am a guest, then I'm free to leave," Brenna asserted, spearing him with a look that dared him to contradict her.

Halvar laughed, a deep sound that boomed in the small area and made her flinch.

"Calder, my brother," Halvar said, still speaking in Brenna's language. "I think she needs to be taught some subservience."

Halvar reached for his loins, his large hand grasping between his legs.

Brenna gasped at the size of what he gripped, though hidden beneath his clothing. She backed up, crawling like the crabs the traders occasionally brought in for dinner, reaching for the wall behind her.

The newcomer—Calder, Halvar had called him—raised his fist and planted it in Halvar's bicep with a resounding smack. "You're scaring her. We agreed. She'd be untouched."

"You agreed, brother." Halvar crossed the space between them swiftly, quicker than Brenna would have thought, and bent, seizing the fabric of her tunic and wrenching her to her feet. Then using his other hand, he rent the fabric, ripping it clear to her waist.

Brenna squealed. One of her hands flew to cover her breasts while the other sought to raise the now shredded tunic. "Animal," she hissed.

"I'll show you an animal," Halvar raised his hand.

Even more quickly than Halvar had moved, Calder was now standing next to him, his large hand wrapped around Halvar's wrist. "Fine then, I agreed. And we lead this tribe equally."

Halvar released a growl and whirled on Calder. "She's a married woman. It is not as though we have to return her untouched. And her father is a lord, her husband a chieftain. Someone will pay her ransom."

Calder jerked Halvar around to face him. "I said no."

Halvar's growl was low. "There are plenty of others." He stomped off.

Brenna regarded the man in front of her. "Thank you," she said, her voice low.

CHAPTER TWO

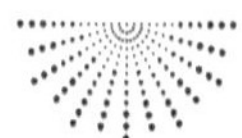

Calder studied the woman before him. Her pale, faultless skin, red hair, and eyes of dark green. He fought the urge to return his gaze to the creamy rose-tipped breasts he'd been given a glimpse of when Halvar had ripped her tunic.

Taking a blanket from the floor, he wrapped it around her shoulders. "I'll have one of the women bring you a change of clothing. You'd be better off not tempting my brother again. His lust is only surpassed by his pride. Women do not reject him."

"I'll reject him with my dying breath," she hissed.

Calder laughed softly at her spirit. "Do not worry, lady; you'll be returned to your husband very soon. He will pay the ransom for a prize like you."

He'd almost said beauty. He gritted his teeth against that. He was not here to befriend her. She was a captive.

She'd provide enough ransom to pay for several ships they'd lost in a storm a month ago.

"My husband—"

There was something in the way she said the words that caught his attention. He appraised her face, flawless, high cheekbones. Eyes wide set. Perhaps not flawless, but he found it to be sheer perfection.

"What of your husband?"

She shook her head and turned away, wrapping the fur tighter about herself.

He'd have sworn he saw a tear slip from those eyes.

Deep in his chest, his bear growled.

Calder ignored the bear. He'd been born a shifter, and his bear was a part of him. His bear was him, and by the same token, he was his bear. And yet...

He and his bear hadn't always agreed.

But at this moment, he found he wholeheartedly agreed with the sentiment his bear was making known. Both of them were attracted to this woman.

He should do as Halvar wanted to do. Plant his root deep in her body to get her out of his head.

He'd been there when Halvar knocked her on the head. Calder had watched over her for three days while she'd lain unconscious, her breathing shallow and her face pale.

In the middle of the night while all others slept, he'd sat next to her in this very cell and run his fingertips chest. Her fur had fallen, her breasts bounced with every strike she laid on him.

"You miserable—you barbarians. You killed all the men? The fathers? The sons?"

He grabbed her arms by the wrists and held them down, then pulled her against his chest, still holding her hands captive.

She struggled against him, deep sobs escaping from her chest.

He put his other hand on her head and let her cry, but refused to release the tiny hammers of her fists, certain they'd be on the attack again.

Finally, she sucked air in deeply and then dropped her head.

A gasp told him she'd discovered she'd lost the blanket covering her breasts, and the plump mounds were against his bare chest.

"If I release you so you can cover yourself, will you stop the assault?"

She nodded, her tearstained cheeks rubbing on his chest.

He let go of her hands. She swooped down and pulled the blanket over her chest swiftly.

"What of the women in the village?"

"They did not perish."

"Did they leave? Are they free or are they captives like me?"

Calder ran his fingers over one of the two braids on

his crown that ran the length of his scalp then cascaded down his back. "They did not leave. And they are not captives like you. Not exactly."

She chewed on her bottom lip, reddening it, making it look as though it had been freshly kissed. "Then exactly what are they?"

"They are here to serve us. They belong to us. You, Lady Brenna, are for ransom. As the visiting daughter of another chieftain—a chieftain from a wealthy area—and the wife of a chieftain, you will garner much silver for us."

"My husband—" Again she stopped short. This time she shook her head. "I'll need to take a bath. I'm filthy. I smell."

"There is no one to attend to you or bring you hot water here," Calder told her. "Tomorrow, you bathe in the river. Under guard, so that we do not lose a precious one like yourself."

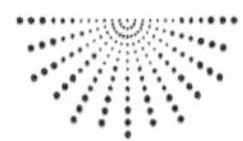

CHAPTER THREE

Brenna didn't sleep that night. Not a wink. A bit after dawn, her barred door cracked open a few fingers' width. She couldn't see who was entering and held her breath hoping it wasn't that scoundrel Halvar, here to finish what he'd started the night before. She found herself wishing it was Calder, but then chastised herself for wanting that barbarian to come in as her savior.

Or more.

She exhaled in frustration at the thought and how much it bothered her.

The door opened farther.

"Astrid!" Brenna exclaimed, though she didn't keep the excitement from her voice, she did keep the volume low. She jumped up from her furs, and wrapped herself in the blanket to preserve her modesty, then leapt into the arms of her cousin.

Astrid had been the one Brenna was visiting.

Astrid wrapped her arms around Brenna, and both women began to sob.

"What happened?" Brenna asked her. "I—I do not remember anything. I think someone hit me."

"Two days ago," Astrid said between sobs, "the raiders came and killed our men. They are ferocious man-beasts."

More like beasts, plain and simple, Brenna thought. "They are animals," she agreed with Astrid.

"Bears. All of them. Shapeshifters, all of them, each and every one."

Brenna stared at her cousin. What was she saying? Did she mean... She didn't want to think of this. By the gods, shapeshifters were the scourge of the north, shifting into an animal form at will. They were the creatures of mythology; tales used to scare children. They weren't—they couldn't be—real.

"No," Brenna whispered. "No, that cannot be."

"But we saw them with our very eyes." Astrid put her hands on Brenna's shoulders and stared into Brenna's face. "Did you not see them? The way they attacked and killed men of the village?"

Brenna shook her head—a head that still ached from the knock she'd received. "I've been—they—someone—hit me. I have not been awake or aware."

"I thought you were dead," Astrid confessed. Tears rolled down her full cheeks. Her lower lip trembled, and her shoulders shook with silent sobs.

The horror was dawning on her, and yet, still in disbelief she began, "They did not..." Brenna couldn't finish her sentence, couldn't speak the horrible words aloud, but she knew the answer.

They had been attacked.

"By the gods," Brenna whispered, "they will pay."

"Who will make them pay? They are more powerful than our gods, or they wouldn't be here doing what they are doing." Astrid took a deep breath, then continued. "They kept the children in the thorn bush corral. They said if the women obey and do as needed, the children will be allowed to live."

"Heathens," Brenna whispered.

Astrid shook her head and was silent, the tears trailing down her face for a spell before she swiped them away with her fingertips. "They sent me in here to give you this." She held out a tunic that Brenna hadn't noticed in her hands. "And I'm to accompany you to the river to bathe."

"They are holding me for ransom," Brenna said.

"I know." Astrid bit her lip. "Eerika told them not to kill you when you attacked one of them with a blade."

"I did that?"

"You do not remember?"

"The last thing I remember, we were preparing for the feast."

"That's when *they* arrived," Astrid told her with a grimace. "You went after one of them with a blade. Sliced his arm. Another one hit you on the head with the back of his axe. He was ready to strike you again, to kill you, when Eerika told him you were valuable. That your husband would pay a lot of money for your safe return."

"And when the truth comes out?" Brenna whispered.

"Eerika was not thinking of that at that moment. Her only wish was to save you from certain death."

Brenna nodded. "Tell her I thank her."

There was a sound at the door, almost a knock, it seemed.

Brenna and Astrid both turned toward the noise.

Calder stood there, an axe in his hand.

Brenna shivered and wondered if he was the one who'd nearly killed her. And for some reason, she hoped not.

"Your bath, lady."

Now she knew why he called her that. But yet, when he said it, it was as though there was mockery in his tone.

"You may bring her to help, if needed." He turned away with a final word. "An assembly of guards will accompany you."

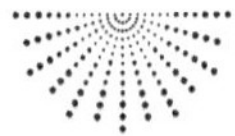

In the hut that held Brenna prisoner, Calder watched her interact with the other woman. He'd actually caught a portion of their conversation. He'd heard Brenna ask what would happen when the truth came out.

He'd not have heard it if he were a mortal man, but being a shifter meant his senses were amplified. He could hear better, see farther, move faster, smell subtleties that most humans couldn't.

What did she mean about the truth coming out? What truth, he wondered.

The two women rose to their feet. The fur blanket was still wrapped around Brenna, in her hand she clutched a new tunic.

The other woman gathered several furs, murmuring,

"You can wrap yourself with these while you dry; the river has not yet begun to warm."

"Thank you, Astrid."

"You'll be going with her to assist," Calder told the other woman.

She nodded after glancing at Brenna.

CALDER, HIS BEST FRIEND GUNNAR, AND TORSTEN— another close ally in the tribe he ruled with his brother, all followed slowly behind the two women as they made their way toward the river.

The path was wide enough for three men to walk shoulder to shoulder, the weeds brushing thighs encased in leggings. The women's long skirts rustled the brush that covered the oft-used path.

Calder hadn't told Halvar he was taking the statuesque red-haired beauty to bathe in the river. He knew that for one reason or another, his brother had a bone to pick with Brenna.

And Halvar was still ensconced in his hut, in the depths of sleep, an arm slung around each of the two village women who lay next to him, all three unclad.

The cabin smelled like sex, making Calder's rod twitch. For too long, he'd been without a woman. It wasn't that he had a problem with taking one of the captives as his own, to bury himself in deeply and release the tension that had built in him.

It was that every time he thought of sex, Brenna's face flashed before his eyes. The image of her countenance while she'd been sleeping, the way her body had risen and dropped with every breath while she'd lain unconscious.

And now that he'd seen at least part of that body, a set of glorious breasts, he couldn't scrub her from his mind. He'd entertained the idea of taking one—or two—of the women to his own hut, but every evening, predictably, after he'd had his dinner, he'd post himself near her door, sharpening his blade, his mind immersed in thoughts of *her*.

Gunnar elbowed him. "We'll be catching a glimpse of her now, won't we. I'd like to see if her hair is as red—"

Calder halted, whirled to face him. "You'll do nothing to jeopardize our getting the ransom from her husband, you understand? Nothing."

Gunnar took a step back from the viciousness in Calder's tone. "I was not going to touch her. Just looking." He held out his hands, palms up. "Just looking."

Calder snorted, then continued to follow the two women. He was angry with himself for having reacted. Since when did he care what his men did with captives?

At the water's edge, Brenna faced the water, away from the men while Astrid helped remove the fur from her shoulders.

Brenna turned to look at the men. "I'd like my privacy."

Torsten guffawed. "She'd like her privacy," he mimicked her.

"Turn around," Calder said.

Gunnar slapped Torsten on the back. "Do as he says." But he gave Calder a questioning look. "And if they run?"

"Where will two women run to that we can't catch them?"

Gunnar laughed.

Calder gave him a pointed look and Gunnar turned his back on the women.

Brenna pierced Calder with a glare, apparently waiting for him to comply.

He scowled and turned.

The soft sounds of splashing told him that Brenna was washing and that he didn't need to turn.

And yet, he did. He couldn't resist. His bear couldn't resist.

Brenna was facing away from him, submerged in water to her neck. Her rich red hair had darkened in the river.

Astrid was facing Brenna and therefore could see that he was watching, but she didn't give him away.

He didn't have a chance to wonder why she kept his secret because just then Brenna rose out of the water and his attention was transfixed. Her long hair covered her back and ended at a set of dimples that served as a crown over a rounded arse and a set of flaring hips.

He held his breath as she ran a cloth over her arms, then Brenna pushed her hair to the side, collected it and wrung it out.

The vision before him was unspeakable.

Calder grunted, then glanced at his cohorts to see if they'd noticed.

Gunnar was watching him with a raised brow.

"Too much ale last night." Calder rubbed his sternum as though he'd just burped.

Torsten nodded sympathetically, as he was always one to put down a bit more ale than the others.

Calder chanced another peek. Her back was still turned.

He regarded the white flesh; it was crisscrossed with angry red slash marks.

Frowning, he turned away from the horrific visage.

Who had beaten her with such fierceness as to break the skin and leave those scars?

Who would whip a married woman?

He wondered how long she'd been married. Had her husband seen those? Had he taken issue with her father for having caused them?

Then it occurred to him. Perhaps it wasn't her father. Could her own husband have done that to her? What man would?

An anger built within him, seething and simmering like stew in the cauldron.

In Calder's mind, his bear roared at the sight of the scars.

CHAPTER FIVE

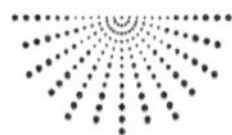

Astrid hissed when she saw the horrific scars on Brenna's back. Brenna herself had seen them in the copper mirror.

"Beast," Astrid exclaimed. "Your husband?"

Brenna nodded. "I'm not anxious to return home." She released her hair to let it cover her humiliation.

"I'd imagine you are not." Astrid scooped water in her hand and poured it over Astrid's shoulder. "Your father, he knows of this?"

"I cannot speak of the shame I endure at my husband's hands." And Brenna could not. The scars on her back were just the beginning of it. How was she to explain that her husband was not fond of her womanhood? Of any woman. He preferred to mount her like a stallion and do to her what she'd witnessed him doing to the stable boy.

locked door in a building made of stone?" Not to mention, she knew Calder had been nearby last night while she'd tried to sleep.

"I did not miss that. We will have to be crafty to set you free. Or pray these men are struck down."

Again, with the striking down part. Brenna exhaled. "Indeed," she said. She had no interest in telling Astrid that no god would be sending lightning bolts to smite their captors.

"Will you get the blanket and hold it for me?" Modesty reigned, and she had no interest in sharing her body with these men. Nor of sharing her secret either.

"Eerika's misdirection will grant us at least ten days. Five for them to arrive at the place she told them you live with your husband, and five to return."

"And then they will know of the treachery."

Astrid nodded.

By the gods, now I have ten days or less to escape these heathens.

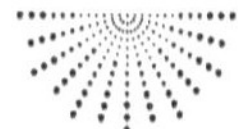

CHAPTER SIX

Calder considered the almost-setting sun. Three days ago, Halvar had sent six men to Brenna's husband to get the ransom. While Brenna had been unconscious the second day, Halvar had cut a lock of her hair and removed a ring from her finger. The six men had taken them as proof so her husband could pay the ransom.

He'd avoided being alone with Brenna since the morning of her bath. The desire in him to ask her about those scars was great. The scars were still angry. Calder visited the healer in his hut, a hut taken over from one of the local villagers.

"Rangan," Calder smiled at the wizened man. "I'm seeking tea tree oil."

"Have you a scar that needs tending?" Rangan frowned. "Let me take care of it."

"No. I'll do it. Do you have any?"

Rangan rummaged through a scarred, old oak chest, then popped up like a rodent from a hole in the ground, a small clay pot in his hands. "Here you are, brother of Halvar."

"I'll return it in a few days."

Calder unlocked the door to the small stone room that doubled as Brenna's cell. He rapped on the door softly with his knuckles before he opened it a crack.

Her "Enter" came seconds later.

She looked at him. Her eyes were clear and vividly green, like precious gems, but glittering as though angry.

"Remove your tunic," he told her softly.

"I will not." She glared at him.

He held up the pot. She frowned.

"For your scars."

Her eyes narrowed even more. "While I bathed. You looked."

He nodded. "I saw nothing. Only the scars." He didn't mention the glimpse of her plump ass or the ivory hips that tempted a man to want to hold them during the act.

She scowled. "I don't believe you."

He shook his head. "Believe what you will." He tilted the pot back and forth. "But this is to help with your scars."

"Leave it with me. I'll have Astrid help me with it tomorrow."

"I can't leave it. If they know I helped you—"

"Then why are you?" Her tone was hostile.

I have no idea.

"Do you want my help or not? Because I will not leave the pot here."

She nodded. "But even more... I'd like your help with..." She chewed on her bottom lip, worrying it so that Calder was sure it would chafe.

He raised his hand and placed the pad of his thumb over her bottom lip and freed it from her teeth. It returned to its place, plump and red.

"Help with what, lady?"

"Please don't call me that."

"Don't call you *lady*? What do your husband's servants call you?

She shook her head. "Don't call me that."

"I shall not, then. What do you want help with?"

"It is close to the solstice, a time I make a wreath in remembrance."

"In remembrance of what?"

"My mother. She passed two years ago."

Calder scowled. He had no idea where to find any such thing as a wreath. "And you want me to fetch you a wreath?"

"I need to collect the plants myself, weave it myself."

Calder pondered this. "It's almost dark. I'll have to

bind you to me. I can't have you running off into the night."

Tears pooled in her eyes, making the green hue glitter more. "I will not run. You can bind me."

He slipped the pot into a pouch at his waist, went outside, securing the cell door behind him then procured a leather strap from near the oxen shed, and returned to Brenna's cell.

"Put your hand out."

He bound her wrist with the strap, then attached it to his own.

He tapped the axe affixed to his belt. "Let this serve as a reminder. Do not try anything, lad—" what was he to call her if not lady? "—woman."

She nodded as though woman was better. Then she said, "My name is Brenna. You know this."

"Brenna," he said her name aloud, the second time ever, though he'd said it in his mind more times than there were stars about.

His reward was a small lift to her lips, a ghost of a smile.

BY THE TIME THE SUN HAD FULLY SET, BRENNA HAD AN armful of flowers and leaves for the wreath she'd be weaving. Calder had walked about with her, patiently attached at the wrists with the strap he'd placed there.

It had occurred to Calder as they'd moved about that it reminded him of a commitment ceremony. His mother had told him his father had been in a commitment ceremony with Halvar's mother first, but she'd died from the winter storm one year, shivering and at the same time burning with a fever, and less than a year later, Aevar had a commitment ceremony with Calder's mother.

Calder's mother died when he was ten, but Calder could remember the stories she'd told him of how she'd met his father, and how they'd been soulspliced. He'd asked her what that was. She said that one day, he'd know. One day, he'd find that woman whose soul was spliced to his.

Calder had grimaced that day and stuck his tongue out as if tasting the most bitter of meads. His mother had laughed. Her laughter brought his father into their great hall to find out the cause of her mirth.

She'd told Aevar that their son found the idea of soulsplicing to be repulsive. Aevar had kissed her on the lips, his eyes gleaming, the ring of gold in his eyes caused by his bear had flickered like firelight.

"One day, he'll know," Aevar had said.

Now both of his parents were gone, and the only one left of his immediate family was Halvar. An older brother whom Calder loved, but had an on and off tenuous and rivalrous existence with, at best.

At that moment, Calder realized that Brenna had stopped moving. She'd been still, and was staring at him.

He locked gazes with her and wished he knew what was on her mind.

CHAPTER SEVEN

Brenna couldn't take her gaze from the man before her. Calder was nothing like the others he traveled with. What was he doing with them? Why did he seem so different?

She studied him.

Was it true he could turn into a bear?

"You have enough for your wreath?" he asked.

"Yes, thank you for letting me collect them."

"The moon is rising." He pointed toward the horizon.

"It's a blood moon." A shiver crossed over her spine.

"Cold?" He raised a brow, took a fur off his shoulders and wrapped it around her.

"Thank you." Brenna didn't want to tell him that the blood moon was a harbinger of bad. Her worry was that it did not bode well. She knew they'd sent the warriors to find her husband and claim her ransom. She'd noticed her hair had been cut close to her scalp at the nape of her neck. She'd also noticed her missing ring.

After Astrid told her they'd taken proof of her abduction, Brenna quickly put together the pieces. She'd not made a fuss, not wanting to attract any more attention from Halvar. She'd kept her presence quiet around Calder's older and more temperamental brother.

"You look worried." Calder tied the fur beneath her chin.

"I am fine."

"Let's get you back. I will apply the tea tree oil, then you can get to your wreath-making."

"Calder?" She touched his shoulder where a tattoo of a large bird met with this chest.

"Hmmm?" He turned to face her, his eyes glowing in the red moon's rays.

"Is it true that you can become a bear?"

He frowned.

"They told me you could."

"Me?" He put a finger on a chest that was broad, muscular, tattooed and scarred. The expression on his face was fearsome.

Brenna swallowed a gulp at the scowl he presented her with.

"I do not know if they said you personally, but you, your group—your men."

Calder nodded. "That's what your village women told you. Do you believe in such foolishness? That men can become beasts? That witches exist?"

She frowned. "Witches do exist. They do. Helga's mother is a powerful witch."

He smirked. "If that be so, then why did your witch not save you? Not save any of you? Not save the men?"

"Freyja is not here. She is out of the village."

"I see."

"Calder!" A voice called from the other side of the brush.

Brenna recognized Halvar's growling, gravelly voice. She flinched and lowered herself closer to the bushes, hiding behind Calder.

Calder gave her a look and slipped the leather strap from his wrist. "Do not go anywhere." He raised a brow then turned toward the sound of Halvar's voice.

"Here, Halvar. Can a man not take a piss without being followed?"

Raucous laughter sounded as Calder headed away from Brenna.

She looked around at the brush, the forest.

Dare she?

The farther away Calder's footsteps sounded, the more her certainty wavered.

It was now or never.

She clutched the wreath's makings close to her chest and ran toward the trees.

She ran and ran, unsure how long she'd run, until she was in such a dense thickness of forest that she could no longer see the moon, nor use its light to guide her.

Winded, with a stitch in her side that was relentless, she leaned against a tree.

"Pssst." A small whistling sound caught her attention.

She looked around the area. Who would be doing that?

Surely it wasn't one of the marauders. They'd have certainly recaptured her, rather than use subtle means to get her attention.

"Who is it?" she whispered into the darkness.

"Is my daughter still safe? I haven't seen her in a day."

"Who are you?"

"Freyja."

"You're back from your trip."

"Keep your voice down, child."

"Sorry. Yes, she is fine. She fell and twisted her ankle. Astrid said she's staying in the cooking hut, keeping the fire going."

"Good. Tell her that in three days, vengeance will be ours. The women are to pick up any weapon they can and attack."

"How will they know when?"

"They'll know."

"Wait, no. I can't go back. I can't. They will kill me when they find out that Eerika—"

A growling, snuffling sound came from nearby.

Brenna gasped. Was that a wolf? A boar? She clung to the tree and gauged the distance to the lowest branch. Could she climb it before the animal attacked her?

She never had a chance to find out.

A hand encircled her wrist.

"I told you to stay put," Calder's voice held admonition. "You could get yourself killed out here. You could have gotten me in trouble." His fingers found purchase on the leather strap and pulled on it.

Brenna was speechless, her mind a flurry of activity, first from Freyja's announcement, then the growling in the trees, and now being recaptured by Calder.

She jerked on the strap. "You don't understand." She hoped Freyja was listening in and could see that one of the enemy was so close.

Enemy? Was he her enemy? *Yes,* she reminded herself. He was her enemy as well as the enemy of her people.

Then why didn't she feel fear with him?

"What don't I understand? That you tried to run away?"

"Your men will kill me when they return from their sojourn."

"And why would that be?"

Tears threatened and then started a treacherous trip down her cheeks.

"They will."

"We'll talk about this after I get you back to your cell. I can't have them noticing that you're missing."

Brenna looked back toward the direction of Freyja but saw nothing. Had Calder not seen or heard them?

He took a step forward, then looked back at her and tugged on the strap.

pondered these questions while his bear paced relentlessly in Calder's mind.

At long last, he asked her a question. "Who put those scars on your back? What did you do to merit them?"

Brenna's head rose slowly from her task at hand, and her eyes took his full measure, then they narrowed, gleaming dangerously in the dim light cast by the candle he'd lit for her. "Who said I merited the scars?"

He tilted his head and pondered her question though she didn't take her gaze from his face. "Who did that to you?"

Her lips turned tight, the bottom lip no longer plump and kissable, but rather a formidable line drawn in the sand.

She opened her mouth to speak but was interrupted by the door flinging open and crashing against the wall.

Three men entered. Three of Halvar's men, not the ones that followed Calder.

"Precious bloom," one of the men slurred.

Calder noted that it didn't take shifter super smelling to scent the odors that wafted from the three intruders. They smelled strongly of ale, and their stumbling was testimony to the amounts they must have consumed.

"Let's see what you have that would make your husband want you back," another one said. His profile was a portrait of pure lust.

"My husband?" Brenna asked. "Did he send word? Did your messengers return?"

The third man laughed. "They shouldn't be back for another two days. Plenty of time for you to heal from tonight's pleasures. Plenty of time." His laugh was raucous and menacing.

"Stay away from me." Brenna pushed herself against the wall and reached for a branch leaning in the corner. She lifted it and was poised, ready to strike.

"Silly wench," the first man said and stepped into the line of fire.

"I will hurt you. I promise."

He stepped even closer.

Probably close enough for her to smell his breath.

Calder was in an awkward position. He knew defending her and hurting his brother's top men would not go over well, but he'd not let this happen.

Seemed his bear had decided the same, but had also determined to take the upper hand.

The man put his hand on Brenna's shoulder and pulled her close.

She struck with the branch, but the man only laughed and yanked it from her.

At this point, Calder couldn't have spoken if he'd wanted to as his bear was in the throes of morphing from Calder's human form into a large dark brown bear.

His muscles stretched, his bones yielded to the shift with a creak.

The men whirled around, hearing his transformation.

It was too late for them to shift into their own bears, though it would have been tight quarters if they had.

Calder rushed them, claws outstretch, he slashed flesh, left, right, back and forth repeatedly. Blood spurted as the men collapsed, all three on the verge of death, bleeding out while Calder's bear stood over them, snarling.

He looked up at Brenna.

She'd fainted and was on the bundle of furs, face up.

Calder pushed against his bear to let him return to his human form, but the bear wouldn't budge. It absolutely refused to yield control to Calder.

So, in his bear form, albeit reluctantly, Calder stood over Brenna, guarding her. He shoved his bear nose against her shoulder and inhaled deeply, his broad bear chest expanding.

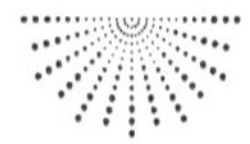

CHAPTER NINE

Brenna opened her eyes. The world before her was dark brown fur.

Fur?

Fur!

A soft growling sound made her heart stop. She froze, motionless, trying to remember.

The fur moved back slightly. Before her on all fours, waited the largest bear she'd ever seen. Bigger than she even thought bears could get.

She wouldn't scream. No, she wouldn't. Screaming might make it attack her.

Then it occurred to her. The bear wasn't acting aggressively. It stood there, watching her. She couldn't help but notice that its eyes, a roasted brown hue had a dark blue ring of flames surrounding the iris.

Just like Calder's but in reverse.

Calder!

She glanced behind the bear, where Calder had been sitting, and of course, he wasn't there. A part of her knew why, but the other part of her was in denial.

It can't be.

She noticed the bodies of men, mauled and bloody, and was relieved that Calder wasn't one of the fallen.

Of course, he isn't, she chastised herself.

And yet...

"Calder?" she whispered.

The bear cocked its head to the side, those peculiar eyes appraising her.

"It's you, isn't it?"

She could have sworn she saw the blue flames flicker.

"You saved me," she uttered.

Then, the dam broke.

Tears came, unfettered, flowing freely.

She swiped them away. No one had ever stood up for her in this way. Never.

"Thank you." She reached out her hand, tentatively, and placed it on the bear's shoulder.

The bear came closer, eclipsing her view of the attackers that had died, hiding the door and its confining bars.

Brenna ran her fingers over the fur; it was thick and almost bristly. She looked into the bear's eyes, and for a reason she couldn't understand, she wanted to tell it—him—about the scars. About her life. About her marriage.

"I'm the second daughter of a wealthy man," she began. "My father isn't a bad person, but my mother died when I was young, and he remarried. After that, his focus was the new woman in his life. I suppose that is how it should be, but to a little girl, it seemed like losing a parent all over again. I felt like an orphan."

Brenna heaved a deep breath at the pain the memories stirred, then continued. "The land between my father's and his enemy belongs to the man I was pledged to. My father arranged the marriage in order to secure the property as a barrier against attack."

Biting back the tears she didn't want to shed, she continued to stroke the bear's coarse fur while he made soft growling sounds that weren't in the least bit threatening.

"My father gave my hand in marriage to a man who prefers men." She hiccoughed the sob back. "He has never taken me as a man would take a woman. He's—" By the stars above, she wasn't sure she could continue. She straightened her shoulders, bolstering herself. "He took me like a man would take another man."

The bear's snarl indicated his understanding and his displeasure.

She lowered her head. "And when I protested, he

whipped my back. Whipped me with the same whip his handlers used on their oxen."

She dropped her head into her arms and hid her face from the shame of it all.

CHAPTER TEN

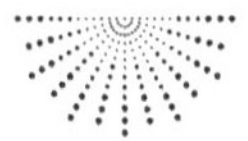

Calder couldn't allow his bear to keep him at bay. He pushed and shoved at his bear's mind until finally, his strength of will won. He rapidly morphed into his human form, ignoring the pain of bones and sinew rearranging, muscles shortening, body transforming.

In his human form, he wrapped his arms around the sobbing woman.

"Brenna," he whispered against her hair, his lips touching her temple. "You shouldn't have gone through that."

I'll kill the bastard, by the gods. I will kill that son of a cur.

She raised her head, emerald eyes glistening. "You're you," her voice was filled with awe.

"Did you doubt it was me?"

"No." Her lower lip trembled. "But—it is so much. Too much. You were a human, then a bear, and now a man again."

"But it is me. It is all me." He placed his fingers under her chin, locked his gaze with hers. "The messengers will be back with the ransom, or your husband, or news. Do you think he will pay the ransom?" He prayed the answer would be no. Then she could be free of the abusive mongrel.

"No."

"What do you mean? Why not?" He fought the urge to jump with joy.

"Because Eerika did not tell them the right place to go. My husband is in the opposite direction. And though he is landed, he has no money. My father paid him to take me because of my husband's lands. That money is long gone. He'd have to go to my father to get the money. He would not do that, even if he knew I was being held for ransom, which he will not know, because your men will return without having found him."

Calder let the information sink in. "That means—"

"That I am worthless to your brother, to your cause. I cannot be used for ransom. Halvar will order my death."

"I will not let that happen."

She was biting the inside of her cheek so hard that he was sure she'd draw blood.

"How could you stop it?"

Calder let out a deep breath, pulled her closer into his arms. "You let me worry about that."

He lowered his head and their lips met.

He claimed her mouth as fiercely as he wanted to claim her body, her heart, her very soul. She belonged to him. To him and his bear.

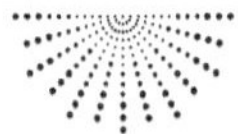

CHAPTER ELEVEN

Brenna restrained a sigh of pure bliss. She'd never been kissed before. Not that she would tell this man so. His mouth devoured hers hungrily, as though he were starving, and the sensation left her tingling and dizzy.

She returned his kiss, savoring the taste and smell of him. Pure man. His hand traveled to the back of her neck, landing gently on her nape, caressing the sensitive flesh there. His other arm curved around her hips, pressing against the small of her back.

His tongue sought hers, seeking, finding, claiming.

Brenna was caught off guard by the arousal he brought out in her. Her body was reaching in ways she had never imagined. Her nipples hardened and pressed against the tunic's fabric, whilst between her legs, a heat grew that left her breathless.

They kissed and kissed while Brenna marveled at the connection a kiss could create.

Calder pulled away, leaving her lips lonely, locking his steely gaze with hers.

"What?" she whispered, astounded at how breathless and husky her voice was.

"I want you. I want you with a ferocity I'd not have thought possible."

"I feel the same," she breathed.

He ran a finger along her jawline, tracing it down, over her neck and into the hollow where she could feel her pulse beating strongly. "Are you saying what I think you're saying?"

She didn't know what the future held, but she knew one thing for certain, she would not rest tonight if it was not in this man's arms, after...

A blush made its way to her cheeks.

"You are embarrassed?"

"Only slightly. I've not... you know my situation."

He nodded gravely. "I won't be rough. I'll have control."

"And if I want you to be rough?" She surprised herself by asking.

"I'll be what you need me to be."

His hands traveled along her waist, pushing the tunic over her ribcage, over her breasts, cupping them at the same time and lowering his head, claiming each pebbled peak, sucking, kissing, licking.

That heat between Brenna's legs grew and her core arched closer to Calder.

He raised his head and she sighed as his thumbs grazed over her dusky nipples, then raised her tunic above her head.

She stood before him, torn between feeling shy and feeling wanton.

"By the gods, you are a goddess." Lust shown in his eyes, and the bear's amber depths flickered within. He threw the tunic aside and slid his hands down, over her hips, cupping her arse, kneading the flesh, tempting the core of her which felt like it had the utmost of sensitivity at that moment, pulsing and throbbing.

Or perhaps that wasn't her pulsing and throbbing alone, for pressed against her was an insistent hardness. His length on her cleft, tempting her with a pleasure she had never experienced.

Brenna wrapped her hands around his neck and pulled him closer, only to find that he was pushing her downward, laying her into the soft furs. She raised herself to her elbows and watched him undress, marveling at the muscles, the rock-hard stomach, the thick legs, and the massive erection between them.

She drew in a sharp intake of breath. He was huge.

He lowered himself, placed a finger over her lips. "Do not be nervous. I would not hurt you."

She nodded apprehensively.

He leaned down, stroking her legs, her stomach, his

When he lowered his mouth and warm air touched a part of her that nothing had ever touched, she flinched as the most delightful of pleasures seared its way along her nerve endings.

"Calder." Her voice was husky.

His only response was to lower his head farther and take her core into his mouth and suck on it gently, at first. Then his sucking grew with intensity as he drew more of her tenderness into his mouth.

She raised her hands, clasped his head, scoring his scalp with her nails while fluxes of pleasure pulsated throughout her being. She ground her body into his mouth, wanting more.

"Greedy," he muttered.

She blushed, felt the heat rising to her cheeks and was thankful that he wasn't looking at her face, that all of his energy and attention was riveted to giving her pleasure.

"I love that you're greedy for me," he affirmed.

She rode more and more waves of sheer desire, surrendering herself to him until all she could do was grab his shoulders and try to pull him up.

Her need for him was overpowering.

He nodded, his face passion filled, his handsomeness rugged, fierce, and filled with promises of a passionate forever.

She wasn't even sure what promises he could make her, a captive, but tonight, she was his, and he was hers.

He rose, his hard body on top of hers as he pulled himself until their lips were touching and his hardness was pressing against a part of her that wanted him so completely.

He rubbed his shaft from her core to her entrance and back, over and over, until she was sure she would scream at him to take her.

And just when she was a breath away from crying out for him, he pressed inward, filling her, slowly, then pushing forward.

Her body took him in as if he were made for her. His width spread her, filling her, touching ever part of her, leaving her breathless, with just a twinge of pain to merge with the pleasure of it all.

Until his first real thrust.

She released a cry. He ceased moving and covered her mouth with his, drinking in her gasp.

Then he raised his head and studied her face. "I'll stop. I did not think it would hurt you so."

"Don't stop." She smiled at him while tears formed in her eyes at his sweetness for worrying about her.

He thumbed a tear away. "You are crying? It hurts this much?"

She shook her head. "Tears of joy. To have a wonderful man like you for my first time." She wondered, too, what the future held. Would they be torn apart when the ruse about her husband was learned? "Please, continue."

He kissed her tenderly. And slid in and out of her, gently, expertly, as if instinctively knowing what to do for her. After several moments of this, he pulled completely out, then plunged in with one long stroke. Over, and over again.

Her body surprised her by delivering more of those waves of pleasure that she rode while she buried her nails in his back. Gasp after gasp, moan after moan, he drove into her, until finally, the wave crested so that she knew she'd be spent, completely and fully.

"Calder! Oh!"

With that, he drove in hard, and she felt a pulsing heat merging with her own. He buried his face into her neck, whispering her name over and over.

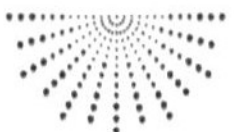

CHAPTER TWELVE

Brenna snuggled deeper into the warmth that surrounded her. The morning sounds from the nearby forest filtered into her sleep-laden mind, but the comfort of her surroundings repeatedly tugged her under, like the whirlpool in the ocean pulled on a swimmer.

She rested her head against a solidness which rose and fell in a rhythm that matched her own breathing. Frowning, still confused, she opened her eyes.

And found herself looking into Calder's eyes with their darker flame that she knew now was his bear. Her lips were tender from a night spent kissing into the early morning hours. Calder had been tender with her, and it was a tenderness she hadn't expected from a man of his people, a man that also was a bear.

Whispers entered her subconsciousness, and for a

brief second, she believed she might be hearing things. Or hallucinating.

Then she recognized the voice.

Freyja!

She listened closely to the words filling her mind, but couldn't understand them. This was not a language native to Brenna. The foreign words were chanted, and they grew louder and louder. Brenna couldn't have said what made her realize that the voices were in her head. The chanting became so loud that it eclipsed her own thinking.

Seconds later, Brenna's world erupted into chaos. The sounds of men yelling, cursing, and women screaming filled the air.

Calder grabbed his head, an expression of sheer pain etched into his handsome features. Tendons on his neck and forehead popped out from the utter agony he was experiencing.

He grunted. "Brenna," his voice was a growl of anguish. "What is happening to me?"

He rose to his feet, barely able to manage that. Brenna stood, put his arm around her shoulders. "I need to get you out of here."

"My bear, something is happening to him."

Brenna gave him a sideways glance. Could she tell him about Freyja? She wasn't sure she could. Then she noticed—

Brenna gasped. "You're bleeding."

Tears of blood flowed down his face.

What was Freyja doing? Would this kill him?

Brenna couldn't have said what instinct drove her next move; she had no experience with witchery or shifters, but somehow, it came to her.

"We have to get you out of here. Away from Freyja. Away from the sound of her chanting voice."

"I hear no chanting. Only yelling and screaming," he managed to say around the cloud of pain that must have ruled his existence at that moment.

"I know. I know you don't hear it, but..." She grabbed his other arm, and tugging him along, pulled him out of the hut.

The village was mass chaos. Men fighting each other, and at the same time appearing to fight ghosts while women came upon them and managed to stab, hit, and club them with anything that could be used as a weapon while the men were incapacitated and holding their heads.

In front of the village's central fire, Freyja stood, clad in a black robe, face upraised, arms lifted to the sky, her lips moved soundlessly. Her eyes were unfocused, looking at nothing in particular.

This was the time. Brenna knew instantly and instinctively she had to get Calder out of there.

Freyja was the most powerful of witches, that was no secret, and whatever she was doing to the men would not end well for them. And by default, that included Calder.

Brenna found herself wishing she had knowledge of how witchcraft worked. How to avoid it, how to circumvent it. But she knew naught about the mystical arts.

She glanced at Calder. Blood streamed from his eyes like uncontained tears of crimson, more than before. She gasped.

He raised a brow. "What is it?"

She shook her head. She couldn't tell him that the bleeding had gotten worse.

"I need to help them." He pointed to his clansmen.

"You can't."

"I must." He made to go toward the melee.

Brenna grabbed his arm, held tightly. "You must come with me. Now."

"Why?" he asked, but he followed her, allowing her to lead him at a sprint, toward a nearby grove of trees.

Once in the cover of the trees, Brenna turned to survey the fracas they'd left behind. More and more of the men had fallen.

"What is happening to my people?" Calder swiped at his face, then stared at his bloody hand. "What in the curses is happening to me?"

"Your people have made a mistake. They've trifled with the wrong witch. This village is one that belongs to Freyja. It's her daughter's village. She's wreaking her vengeance on your kind. The others will not survive. I need to help you."

He shook his head. Blood flew from his face. "No. I have to help my brother. My men."

"No." She refused to release his arm. "For the sake of our baby."

He scowled. "What is this madness you speak of, woman? You cannot know you are with child the next day after a coupling."

She would have to tell him about her dream. She hadn't really had a chance to process the meaning herself yet.

"We will have a son. He will be the start of a new breed of people. I will not let you put that in jeopardy."

"Are you saying..."

She shook her head. "I do not know what I am saying. I do not know if the gods are revealing a child that will come this year or in the next few years. All I know is that we are destined."

Calder put his hands on her face, cupping her cheeks, his eyes locked with hers. "I know not of what you speak, woman. I only know that my heart calls for you. My mind calls for you. My bear needs you."

Brenna tried not to let her emotions get carried away. This wasn't the time to tell him how much he meant to her. How he'd become engrained in her very soul. "Then you must come with me. You must let me save you."

He gave her a nod and they took off at a sprint with only the clothes on their bodies, an axe in his hand, a knife in hers. She led him to a mountain, winding their way up, she knew of a cave, one she'd found ages ago when she'd visited the village as a young girl and explored the area.

At the cave's entrance, she paused. "This is where we will stay." She thought for a moment, then added, "For now."

He was pale, the hand holding the axe shaking.

She led him into the depths, sitting him against a wall. Uncertain what to ask or how to say it, she relayed what was on her mind. "What is it that you're feeling?"

"That my bear is chained. He cannot come forward. I cannot shift into my bear." He leaned forward. "I'll start a fire."

She stayed his hand. "No. Not until we know we are safe."

"Safe from whom?"

"From the other women. From Freyja." She didn't want to tell him that the other men would be dead without a doubt, including his brother.

"They are mere women," he scoffed.

"You'd be ill-advised to think they are mere anything. You know not who Freyja is."

His chest puffed out in defiance, his jaw set firmly.

"Please, Calder. Please, listen to me."

He gave her a nod.

"I'll be back," she told him.

"Where are you going?"

"Just to the entrance." She hadn't told him she'd

heard a noise behind them. She didn't tell him she wondered why his inner bear had not picked up that there was someone—or something—following them. "I won't be long."

"Don't go far." His eyes fluttered closed, his face a visage of pain.

"I won't." She wiped the blood from his cheeks with her sleeve.

She picked up the axe he'd set nearby, and with one final glance in his direction, she made her way toward the entrance.

Brenna hadn't been wrong. There was someone following them. She caught a glimpse of a shadow moving within the trees not far from the entrance. Moving to the side of the entrance, she made her way out, and circled around to behind where the shadow had last been.

A tiny sound, a leaf being crushed beneath a careful footfall alerted Brenna. She whirled around, the bladed weapon in her hand at the ready, raising it above her shoulder, poised to strike.

Just as Brenna was bring the weapon down on the figure that had stepped out of the trees' cover, she froze.

"Eerika," Brenna hissed.

Eerika's eyes were wild. "Hush. One of them escaped."

Brenna narrowed her eyes. "What do you mean?"

"One of those bastards. He came this way. He's not

traveling alone. He's with—" Eerika paused. Her eyes took in the axe Brenna wielded.

Brenna knew she could see this belonged to one of the captors, it was clearly of their people.

Next, Eerika's gaze traveled to Brenna's bloody sleeve. Her stare turned hard and cold. "You are..." She rubbed at her head. "You're not traveling with..."

Brenna dropped the axe and pulled the knife from her hip and lunged forward. "Say no more."

"You'd kill me?" Eerika's voice was tinged with incredulity.

"I owe you my life for the lie you told when they were going to kill me."

Eerika licked her lips nervously, her eyes dropping to the blade at her throat. "How do you know about that?"

"Astrid told me. I owe you. Take yourself away. Now."

"But..." Eerika's head tilted inquisitively. "You are harboring him?" Horror was etched in her features. "Why? Did you not see what his people did to us?"

"His people. Not him. Calder is different."

"You trust me not to go back to the village and get the women? We could outnumber and overpower you."

Brenna nodded. "I realize this. I do. But I know you won't do that."

"How do you know?"

"Astrid. We both love her. We wouldn't put her in a position to choose between our friendships."

Eerika's anger and concern faltered. "True." She

glanced around Brenna, toward the cave's entrance. "You love him?"

I do. More than life itself. But it was so much more than that for Brenna. Mere love did not convey the depth of the emotions she felt for Calder. "He is my destiny."

CHAPTER THIRTEEN

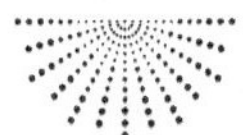

Calder couldn't explain what was happening within him. His bear growled and snarled like a beast in chains. Calder remembered seeing a bear like that once, long ago. A traveling band of entertainers had been going through the village Calder lived in with his family.

The travelers had a captive bear they used for entertainment. It was easy to see that said amusement was based on the cruelty they exhibited on the bear to make it appear fierce to the audience. The bear's body and face were covered in scars and burnt tissue.

Calder had seen twelve summers, maybe thirteen when he first caught glimpse of the bear. He'd complained to his father, telling the older man that he wanted to save the bear, to release it from bondage.

His father had scolded him and reminded him that

that. It wasn't as if the bear could get out of the cell and retrieve it, or even have the manual dexterity to use it.

Calder wondered if perhaps his paranoia had gone too far. He rushed toward the key, slipped it off the peg and was in front of the bear in seconds.

"Here we go." He unlocked the chain and beckoned the bear forward.

The bear snuffled and studied Calder for what seemed like an eternity while it made up its mind.

Then, taking one ambling step after another, the bear made its way out of the cell, tentatively, as though not believing it actually could leave the iron bars behind.

"Come on," Calder whispered. "We need to get you out of here."

And get him out of there, Calder did. They made their way toward the forested area that bordered on the town, and then Calder led the way into the depths of the shadows, where he shifted into his bear.

Together, Calder and the bear explored the forest, taking down a deer, enjoying the fresh warm meat in the icy temperatures of that far northern climate.

For three days, Calder led the bear farther and farther away from humanity and the dangers that people brought to his kind.

Finally, mission accomplished, the bear free, and Calder's heart at peace, the boy made it home.

Sadly, what awaited Calder was a whipping at a post not unlike the one that held the key.

His father's hand was heavy as he laid the leather straps into his son's back until blood was drawn.

"You do not disobey me," his father had said.

"How did you know?" Calder said between unshed tears. He'd refused to let the tears flow. "How did you know I was—what I did?"

For it was not unusual for Calder and his brother to occasionally vanish on hunting trips—together or separately—and return days later. Their father had never been concerned before, as bear shifters, they were perfectly capable of caring for themselves.

His father's smile was grim. "I can smell the bear on you."

And so, the bear he'd saved had inadvertently betrayed Calder. But neither Calder, nor his bear, had regretted the act they'd committed in saving the other animal.

It was that other bear's confinement that brought Calder's circumstance to his mind. His bear was as captive in Calder's mind as that bear had been in its cell.

What is happening to me?

Calder knew it had something to do with witchcraft. What else could it be? What else could make all the men in his clan have the same symptoms? Were the men alive? Was Halvar? Or Gunnar, Torsten?

Calder had to get to them. To help them, but at the moment, he couldn't move. His bear was chained within his mind, but something had paralyzed his legs. He couldn't feel them. How did that happen? When? Was it related to his bear? He opened his eyes, and found himself encased in darkness so dark as to be midnight black.

What is this?

Even in solid darkness, he could see because of his shifter vision. Why could he see nothing now?

He raised his arms—at least he could do that—and rubbed his eyes. Still the same darkness persisted.

Have I gone blind? Permanently?

It was with these thoughts that Calder's mind was plagued when the same darkens took him into a state of unconsciousness, his bear taking him into a shared blackness.

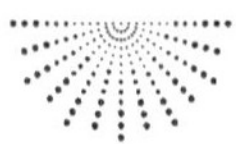

CHAPTER FOURTEEN

Brenna returned from her talk with Eerika to find an unconscious and pale Calder.

Her first thought was that they would need food. He would especially, because he'd lost blood, and not just a little.

Anguish tore at her. She'd have to leave him. She couldn't hunt and kill something with what they had. An axe and a knife wouldn't serve. Given enough time, perhaps she could make a trap, but...

No, time was not on their side. She had to make sure he could eat, and then they would have to vacate the area. They couldn't stay here.

Though Brenna trusted Eerika to keep her secret, she couldn't risk having another person happen on them.

She exhaled her frustration. There was really only one option: go to the village and take some food.

She appraised Calder, wondering if what she was doing was right.

No, she didn't second-guess her desire to be with him. What she questioned was how she was going about this. Would he be incapacitated? Would she be able to fend and hunt for them?

She pushed the nagging doubts aside. One thing at a time. First, food. And with that thought in mind, she placed the axe next to him, secured her knife at her hip, and left the safety of the cave for the unknown status of the village.

THE BATTLE BETWEEN THE VILLAGE WOMEN AND THEIR captors had ended, and the women had been triumphant.

From the cover of the brush, Brenna noticed how the women, victorious and celebrating, had painted their faces with dye, creating runic symbols on their bodies and limbs.

She heard the word Valkyrie mentioned repeatedly, and caught sight of Freyja, striding from woman to woman, looking much like a general on the battlefield.

The women had freed the children from the thorn corral and were dragging the bodies of the dead men to the same thorny enclosure, in the interim piling wood on the bodies.

Brenna shook herself from her reverie. There was no time to study the happenings here. She had a purpose. She noted one of the storage huts, the one closest to the forest. She could slip in there. It was close to dusk, she might be able to do so unnoticed, and grab enough food for—well, she'd grab as much as she could because who knew how long they'd be unable to hunt and cook.

With stealth and surefootedness she'd have never thought herself of, Brenna managed to find a bag and fill it at the hut. Just as she was leaving, she spied anther bag. She took the first one and secured it in a branch on a tree then ran back to the hut to get the second bag.

The sun had fallen, the woods were dark, and the sky ominous, but the village was well-lit for a pyre had been set, using the wood and the bodies of the dead captors.

The stench was overwhelming, and brought to mind another time when her father's family had done the same to an uncle that had passed. That smell. Her stomach roiled.

Leaving the first bag in the tree, well hidden by branches she'd arranged carefully, Brenna took the second bag and made her way toward the cave, stumbling about in the dark, wishing she had better night vision.

She scoffed at that, and of course, it made her think of Calder and how well he could see in the dark.

"Where have you been?" a voice said in the darkness of the forest.

She gasped. Her heart leapt into her throat. And then she recognized the voice.

"Calder. What are you doing out here?"

"I could ask you the same."

"I had to get us food. How are you?" She wished she had enough light to see his face, to ascertain he was doing better.

"I am conscious. Was I out long? Days?"

"No, no. Not days. Just a few hours."

"You went back to the village?" He took the bag from her shoulder.

She heaved a sigh of relief at not having the weight on her back.

"I did."

"My—my brother? My men? My clansmen?"

She bit her lip. She didn't want to say.

"I can smell them," he told her. "I'm just wondering if you saw—" His voice broke. "Mostly my brother, Gunnar, Torsten?"

She swallowed hard. "I did not see any of them. No one I recognized, but..." She swallowed again. "I didn't see anyone alive."

He cursed softly in the darkness, then took her hand. "Follow me. I'll lead us back to the cave."

NEXT TO CALDER, HER HEAD AGAINST HIS CHEST, BRENNA

chewed on dried meat. "I'll fill the water bag from the creek in the morning."

"I need to see for myself."

She knew what he meant. But she didn't want him going there. What if Freyja had put a ward of protection over the village? What if he lost his life just to see if anyone survived?

"You shouldn't."

His chest rose abruptly, then fell as he exhaled mightily. "I must. If there is anything…"

"Calder, Freyja is a powerful sorceress. She overpowered your entire group. All those men. You think she will have a problem with you?"

"I must see." His voice reminded her of the hardness of the rock wall behind her, of the inflexibility of his axe.

MORNING BROUGHT AN ANGER TO BRENNA WHEN SHE realized the spot next to her was empty. She found her fury burning deeply within. How could he leave? How could he go to check on them and risk his life to do so? Did he not understand there was imminent danger for him at the village?

These were the very thoughts that consumed her when the very cause of her angst walked into the cave's entrance and made his way back to her. He carried two water bags, and his face was free of blood, as was his clothing, though it was dripping wet.

"You should not have done that." She fumed.

He leaned in, kissed her on the lips. A part of her softened, his lips were cool and tender against hers. "I had to go check on my brother, my men."

There was a sadness in his eyes that told her not to ask any questions.

He handed her the bag with water.

"Thank you."

He nodded. "We cannot stay in the area."

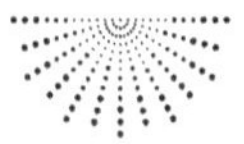

CHAPTER FIFTEEN

It had not been easy to see the bones of so many he'd known and fought next to in the ashes of the pyre the women had created.

He overheard the powerful one called Freyja telling the women they were now a new breed. That they were Valkyrie. And that they were to be warriors.

Though Calder knew and understood the life of a warrior, he'd never taken into account there could be an army of women warriors.

A part of him wanted nothing more than to shift into his bear and wreak havoc and seek vengeance upon these village women who now strutted, carrying weapons, occasionally mock-sparring.

Was this how his own men had behaved in front of the women? Is that why they were doing this? Was this what they had seen modeled and were now emulating?

In his head, Calder's bear roared, mourning the other bear shifters, their bears, particularly. Calder wondered if the anguish his bear felt would allow him to break the chains that bound him, rendering him unable to shift into his bear. And knowing that he risked discovery, Calder pushed for a shift.

He pushed, he strained, and yet, nothing could break the invisible bonds that bound his bear into powerlessness.

And so, it had been that Calder had left the site of the village and gone to the water to fill the bags and return to the woman who'd saved his life.

It was with this in mind, he watched the woman he'd come to love more than life itself drinking the water he'd brought, and told her, "We cannot stay in the area."

Brenna nodded, her face tear streaked through the grime and blood of the prior day's events. "I know not where we can go."

"We could go to my father's people."

He knew instantly that had been the wrong thing to say from the paleness that had drained her cheeks.

"I cannot fathom living among the types of—" Brenna placed the water bag down. "The men who did what they did to that village are not the type I want to be around."

He nodded. "You know that I am—was one of them."

"You are different," she said with vehemence.

This was true. Now. But, surely, she knew he had a past. "I am, now."

She was shaking violently.

He took her in his arms.

Brenna sunk into him and he gave her comfort and assurances into the night that he was a different man. All the while, wondering what had happened to his bear and if it could be reversed.

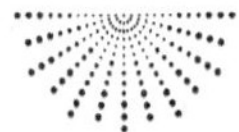

CHAPTER SIXTEEN

A few short winters later.

Brenna pushed her hair from her face and ran after her three-year-old son, Gunnar. On the way, she cast a dirty look in Calder's direction, only to find her mate laughing softly.

"Oh, you think it's funny the way this young man keeps his mother on her toes?"

Calder dropped the blade he'd been using to skin a deer he'd brought home and with several long strides swooped a giggling Gunnar into his arms, then tossed him upward.

Gunnar released a high squeal of excitement and demanded his father do it again, and again.

Brenna sat on a stump near them, breathless. Her

inside kicking, she knew she had exactly what she wanted.

LITTLE DID SHE EXPECT THAT PEACEFUL, HAPPY LIFE TO BE disrupted one day when a large, grimy man in rags and long hair, with tattoos on his face emerged into the clearing where she was hanging the baby's clothing.

She'd given Calder another son, and she'd told him to name this one too, as she would name the girls when the time came, if they should have girls. She'd known that it meant much to her mate to give names to the children that would honor the men in his tribe and those in his family.

And she'd not been surprised when he'd named the next child Torsten. She'd wondered why he hadn't named them after Halvar, his brother, but she wasn't sure of the ways of his people.

The grimy, filthy man with wild eyes stared at her as if she were an apparition.

She bit back a scream and was thankful her children were both napping in the cabin.

But Calder was out getting water. And she was here alone. With this man with wild eyes and a strange demeanor.

She grabbed for the hatchet Calder had fashioned

for her to keep at hand, one large enough for self-defense, but not so unwieldly as the one he sported for himself.

The man released a growl as he approached.

She raised the hatchet. "Stay back."

"I know you," the man snarled.

"Go away," she warned him with a thrust of the hatchet.

He wasn't close enough to strike, but she wasn't sure she wanted to allow him to be.

A crunching to her left almost made her look. Almost. But she kept her eyes on the man.

Did he have friends? Would she be under attack from several of them? She took small sideways steps to get between the stranger and their cabin.

"Go," she snapped, still keeping her eyes on the man.

Then came the last sound she wanted to hear.

"Mama?" Gunnar's voice came from behind her.

"Stay there, Gunnar," she cautioned her son.

"Gunnar?" the wild man said.

"Halvar?" Came from her left where she'd heard the crunching.

Except that was Calder's voice. She cast a sideways glance. Calder was staring at the man.

Wait. He'd said, Halvar. That was the name of Calder's brother.

She stared at the man. Could it be?

It was!

Calder came running toward the large man and enveloped him in a bear hung. "Halvar! I thought you'd perished."

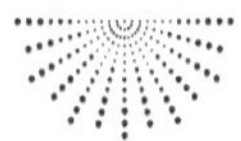

CHAPTER SEVENTEEN

Calder held Halvar at arms' length, his hands on his brother's shoulders, and he took stock of the man he'd thought dead, and hadn't seen in so long—since that day, that fateful day.

Tears streamed down Halvar's cheeks, leaving light streaks on his grimy skin.

Calder was speechless. In all the years, he'd never seen his brother cry. Never seen a sign of weakness. He'd not always agreed with Halvar's ways or decisions, and definitely didn't share his ethics in certain areas, but he loved his brother and respected his military acumen.

Seeing Halvar cry touched a part of Calder he didn't know he had.

He pulled Halvar in close, hugging him fiercely. "Where have you been, brother?"

Halvar coughed, cleared his throat and pulled away,

swiping his cheeks with pawlike hands, leaving horizontal stripes across the vertical steaks, making a crisscross pattern on his face.

"I escaped the hell that witch rained down on our men. She killed our bears. Or at least, she may as well have. None of us could shift. My bear has fallen silent, imprisoned as if he's encased in a box of ice."

Calder nodded glumly. He knew all about that. He'd still not been able to free his bear. This failure tore at him daily, hearing his bear's mournful call for release, but being powerless to free him, powerless to shift into his bear.

Halvar studied his face. "And your bear?"

Calder shook his head. "The same as yours."

"It was that cursed witch, she cursed us. All of us. And she—" Halvar pointed at Brenna, "she is one of them. She is behind this as well. Just as guilty as the witch."

Calder shook Halvar's shoulders lightly. "She is not, brother. She saved my life."

Halvar scoffed and appraised Brenna through narrowed eyes where she stood at the cabin's entrance, Gunnar peeking from between her legs.

Calder pulled Halvar's attention back to him with another shake. "Listen to me. She is my woman. The mother of my sons. She saved me. She can come to no harm."

Halvar frowned. "Gunnar, the boy she called to… that is your son?"

"As is the infant. Torsten. The next one would be named Halvar."

A grim smile curved Halvar's lips upward, slightly, as though hesitant to give much emotion away. "And you say she's a good woman? She saved you?"

"Indeed."

"Maybe I should reconsider my opinion of her."

Calder didn't tell his brother that for his own sake, it would be best if he did. Harboring ill will toward Brenna would not bode well in Calder's home. He'd not be able to harbor his brother and give him a place to stay if he warred with Brenna, for Calder's allegiance was firmly with his woman. "That would be good," he told his brother. "How did you manage to escape?"

"I don't know. I was not in the village. I'd got to the woods, and suddenly, was just leaving the cover of the trees when the pain struck me." Halvar grabbed his head, as though reliving the pain.

Calder remembered that agony only too well.

Halvar continued, "I collapsed. I lost consciousness. When I awoke, the men were dead, they were being burned, and my bear was lost to me forever. I thought I was the only survivor."

"Brenna pulled me out before they could kill me. Those women—"

Halvar grunted. "Valkyrie, they called themselves." He cursed under his breath. "One day, we shall be avenged. In the name of bear shifters, in the name of our tribe, one day…"

"Valkyrie." Calder didn't tell his brother he knew that name. Didn't tell him that, though he never discussed it with Brenna, he daily cursed the Valkyrie and prayed to the gods that vengeance would belong to his people. "Brenna took me from the foray, hid me in a cave, helped me heal. We have been together since."

"You have feelings for her?" Halvar raised a brow. "Or are you with her because you are beholden to her for your life?"

"She's my mate. Fated to be mine. There's never been a doubt in my mind, and there was no doubt in my bear's mind when he was not—when he was himself."

"So, you had feelings for her when she was our captive."

"Aye, brother. I did."

Halvar nodded as though this admission explained a lot to him. Maybe it did, Calder figured, studying the fire that would need to have more wood put in it. Maybe now Halvar would understand some of Calder's protectiveness of her.

"And her husband?" Halvar asked.

Calder snapped his head back to his brother's face. "Her husband is not an issue. He never has been."

Halvar's brow flew upward. "Until he finds out she exists?"

Calder shrugged the question off. He didn't tell Halvar how close they were to her father's lands. How this could happen if she went into a town. If she were to be amongst others.

"Why have you not taken her north? To our people? To our father?"

Calder grimaced. "She does not have good memories of encounters with our people."

"Ah, pity that. Our people have a long and proud heritage." Halvar gave his own shrug. "She is your woman. You tell her what to do. You make the decisions."

"That is not my way."

"That is the way of our people. She is merely a woman."

"I have to do what is right for both of us." Not to mention Calder didn't want to remind his brother that women were not to be underestimated. He'd witnessed that firsthand. So had Halvar. But there was no reason to rub salt into that wound.

"Perhaps I should get to know this woman better. I may have underestimated her. I'd like to get to know my nephews as well."

Calder glanced back at the cabin's open doorway where Brenna still watched them, her face expression-less. He beckoned her forward. She pushed Gunnar toward the inside of the cabin and closed the door behind her, then approached Calder and his brother, a half-smile on her face.

By now, Calder knew that was her look of uncertainty. He didn't fault her for that.

CHAPTER EIGHTEEN

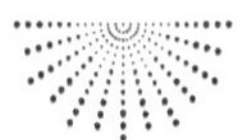

Brenna still harbored resentment for Halvar. She knew she shouldn't. As she took slow, measured steps toward Calder and Halvar, she determined that she should be the better person. She should be forgiving of others.

But by the love of all she held holy, she could not. Not easily. She took a deep breath, letting the crisp air fill her lungs. Winter was upon them. She and Calder would have to work extra hard. She didn't want to tell him that she was with child again. Already. So soon after Torsten's birth.

She hoped for a girl, because one day, that meant she'd have more help of the kind she needed. They didn't need more hunters. She needed help with a woman's work. And though Calder often offered to help.

He was all thick fingers and thumbs when it came to doing some of the tasks she wanted help with.

She let the breath out slowly as she reached Calder and Halvar. "Greetings," she said in the language Calder had been teaching her.

Halvar beamed a joyous smile, looking at his brother. "You've been teaching her our language."

Calder nodded.

"You are welcome to our abode and our fire," Brenna told him.

"Thank you." Halvar cast his eyes downward, as though ashamed of...

What, she wondered. *What is he ashamed of?*

Though truthfully, she could think of many things this brutish cad of a man could be ashamed of, she doubted he had the depths and character to recognize it.

Halvar looked up and locked gazes with her. "I have not always been a good man. And I was not fair to you."

She bit back a gasp. *Wonders would never cease.* The man did have an understanding of his wrongdoings. Unless Calder had something to do with it. She glanced sideways at Calder. But no, she didn't think Halvar's response was spurred on my her mate. The man had experience an awakening, it seemed.

"I am glad to see you are well."

"It is no thanks to your kind," he snapped, then clamped his lips together tightly.

"You do not think your kind did anything to merit the actions taken against them? Killing the village's men? Raping their women?" Maybe she'd been wrong. Maybe he hadn't learned anything.

His jaw worked, the muscles tensing then releasing before he finally replied. "I misspoke. My apologies."

Brenna noted the sincerity in his tone and the concern on Calder's face. Though she did not want to relent and be forgiving, her heart told her she should be more accepting. That Calder could have insisted she be among his own kind, but he'd never pushed the matter.

He'd never asserted that they move to the north, rather he'd been content to remain in this area and make a home with her. And by the same token, she'd never pressed him to join her people—though for her it would have been more difficult since she was legally still bound and wed to her husband.

No, she could not harden her heart. She needed to forgive Halvar—for her husband's sake. As well as for the sake of her children.

Brenna took Halvar's hand in hers. "There is nothing to forgive, brother."

Calder put his arm around her and drew her against his body. She knew she'd done the right thing.

She tugged on Halvar's hand. "Would you like to meet your nephews?"

"Indeed, I would."

Brenna squeezed Calder's hand. He gave her a look of appreciation. She nodded her acknowledgment.

Halvar was in front of the fire, playing with Gunnar, telling him stories about bear shifters. Stories that Calder had never told the child out of respect for Brenna's feelings on the matter.

Halvar, who had no knowledge of this, was regaling the little boy with his tall tales.

Brenna hadn't put a stop to it. She believed Gunnar would forget about the stories. He was so young still. If he never heard about them after this night, once Halvar was on the road, she could make sure they were never brought to his attention again.

Gunnar's eyes grew droopy, his lids falling, though he fought to keep them open.

Halvar held him out for Brenna to take. She held her little son, kissing his forehead, then looked at Halvar, who bore a tender expression on his face.

Brenna made a snap decision. "Stay with us for as long as you want."

Emotions flooded Halvar's face. "Thank you."

With a final glance at her mate, she nodded and took Gunnar to the cabin where baby Torsten was already fast asleep.

The image of Calder's appreciation for the gesture

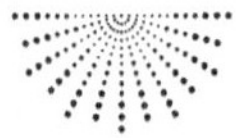

CHAPTER NINETEEN

Calder frowned at Halvar. "Help you with what?"

"My bear, it's gone mad. It keeps trying to kill me. Are you not suffering from this?"

Calder poked at the fire with a long stick, watching the sparks he created fly upward above from the flames. "No. My bear is chained, but he does not try to kill me."

"Mine is always trying to kill me or to get me killed. Always."

"How does he try to get you killed?"

"He pushes me into fighting. It's as if a madness sets in and this great rage is in control of me. I can't seem to stop it. And before I know it, I'm usually embroiled in a fight with anyone I run into." Halvar pushed his unkempt hair away from his face. "I no longer go around others. I stay in the woods. Killing what I need, eating from the land, occasionally stealing if I must."

Sadness overtook Calder. "That is no way to live, brother."

"I know this."

"Why have you not returned home? To our people? To seek help? Perhaps a cure?"

"You think I did not?" Halvar rose and began to pace tight circles in the firelight. "I headed directly for our people. I traveled months by foot. I was but a few days away when I ran into our cousins, Bjarke and Audun."

Calder nodded. He knew those names. "What happened?"

"I told them everything. They said that I was no longer one of them. That I was cursed, and cursed ones did not belong amongst our people. They tried to kill me."

Calder hit his forehead with his palm. Those stupid ignorant bastards.

"I killed them," Halvar said with a whisper. "It was not what I wanted, but I had no choice."

Calder did not blame his brother. He'd have done the same if his cousins tried to kill him. "Understood."

Halvar stopped pacing to lock gazes with Calder. "I knew then I could not go back. I should not have suggested earlier that you return home. I did not understand that your bear has gone as well. Consider yourself lucky that he doesn't try to kill you."

"What is it that you want my help with?" Calder

wondered if his brother needed a weapon or clothing, or a place to stay.

"I need you to help me die."

"Help you die?" Incredulity and horror colored Calder's voice. "I cannot do that. You know I cannot."

"You must." Halvar dropped to his knee in front of Calder, taking his hands in his. "You must release me from this hell I'm in."

"That is a depravity I will not commit." Calder's jaw muscles were taut with tension. "You cannot ask me for that."

Despair and hopelessness filled Halvar's face. "I think the day has been long enough."

Calder rose to his feet, put a hand out to help his brother up. "Come to the cabin, sleep in comfort."

"I prefer the open air now. I no longer can sleep under a roof. Maybe if you have a fur or two that you can spare?"

"Of course, but you are not leaving in the morning light, are you?"

"That I am not." Halvar's smile was grim.

CHAPTER TWENTY

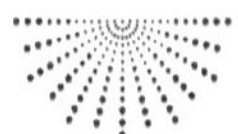

Several cold nights later.

Calder couldn't have said what woke him. One moment he was asleep, an arm flung around Brenna, the next he was sitting upright, his heart pounding.

Except, it wasn't only his heart. It was his bear too. His bear, though silent, though chained, was in a state of panic.

This was a new sensation for Calder. He rose to his feet, making sure Brenna was snug under the covers, and reached for his boots, then his axe.

Slipping outside, he noted the fire was still in a roar. Halvar had never come inside to sleep, preferring to spend his nights outside under the sky, always keeping the fire going.

across her high cheekbones, her plump bottom lip, and thin upper lip.

He'd wondered about her name, wondered much about her. Was she a mother? Was she happy with her husband?

While she was unconscious, she didn't speak, didn't call out the name of any man. Wouldn't she have called out the name of her husband if...

He pushed those fruitless thoughts away. He should not have spent those nights watching over her. He should not have let his bear begin to have feelings for her.

Yes, he should rut to get her out of his system. But he wasn't sure that would do it. He'd only want her more, he suspected.

She turned to face him. "What of the others? From the village?"

"What is your name?" he asked.

"Brenna."

"Brenna," he repeated, liking the sound of it as it rolled off his tongue.

"The others? The villagers?"

He clenched his jaw. She would not like the answers, of that he was certain. "The men fought bravely."

Her eyes widened. "You killed them?"

"They died in battle."

She threw herself at him; her hands beat on his

It had been a rude awakening for her when she'd discovered her husband preferred not to sleep with women. That he did what he did to her out of anger.

Her father would do nothing to help her, this Brenna was sure of. Her husband held the land between her father's lands and her father's enemies. He'd never risk losing the advantage by calling Brenna's matrimony null. Never.

"And so you will suffer? Endlessly?"

Brenna nodded. She felt Calder's eyes on her. And had no doubt it was him. She didn't want to turn his way so he wouldn't know she was aware of him. She hoped he hadn't seen her back. And then she wondered why she cared.

"And what of you?" Brenna changed the subject. "How are you faring in our new wardens' hands?"

"My wish is that they will be stricken down by the hands of the gods."

Brenna had stopped believing in the gods. She believed in nothing but had no wish to dispel Astrid's hopes. "Let us hope."

Astrid leaned in. "Last night, they asked Eerika where your husband was. She told them to the east."

Brenna sucked in air. "But—"

Astrid frowned at her. "I know. This will buy time."

"Time for what?"

"Time for you to live. To escape."

"Escape? Did you miss that I am kept behind a

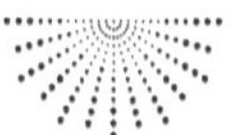

Calder situated Brenna in her cell. He hadn't said a word to her on their trek back. She'd stumbled the entire walk as they returned, and even asked once why he didn't.

He hadn't been about to tell her that shifters could see in the dark.

She sat in the corner, on a pile of rugs, and sorted through the plant life she'd collected for her wreath making, then she began to plait and weave the components. Brenna never once looked up at him.

Calder dragged a seat to the opposite corner, one where he could see who would enter before they could see him. And he watched her, this strong, silent beauty who'd dared to run. Why had she returned so easily? Why hadn't she struggled or tried to escape? He

fingertips making patterns over her flesh, threatening to consume her with a desire unlike one she'd ever thought existed. She ached for him. An ache evident in the soft moans that escaped her lips. In the center of her cleft, a sensation of a current running through her made her moans turn to panting.

While exploring her body, he lowered his lips to hers, his tongue taking hers in a primal dance that left her head spinning. He lowered his head, his tongue sliding between her breasts, licking the valley between, then worshiping her nipples while his large hand cupped and hefted the weight of her breast, making sounds of approval that spurred her passion higher.

He lapped and licked at her hardened peaks while she felt a moisture building within and her muscles contracted, over and over, wanting him within her.

He raised his head, studied her face. "You are the most beautiful woman." His voice was not much more than a growl, his bear close to the surface.

He lowered his face, tracing a trail from the valley between her breasts to her stomach.

And lower.

Lower.

Lower.

Brenna held her breath.

He placed his hands on either side of her mound, and spread her open.

She gasped at the excitement this brought her.

they did not interfere in the goings-on of humans. That the bear was not a shifter, nor was it human. It was merely a beast. This answer did not satisfy Calder, who against his father's orders, in the still of the night with the snow falling, slipped out of the warmth of his bed and the security of his father's cabin, into the cold night.

Finding his way in the dark, his shifter vision enabling him to see clearly even on this moonless night, Calder found the bear. The creature was hungry and miserable, and Calder's heart broke to witness this.

A large padlock served as the obstacle that would allow him to remove the chain that held the bear prisoner in a cell too small for the beast to even stand in.

A key. That's what Calder needed. A key to free the bear.

"I'll be back," he whispered to the bear, who seemed to understand that Calder was not the foe, and watched the young human with curious dark eyes.

Calder expected to hunt a key, to have to pilfer through possessions and tents. What he did not anticipate was that he would actually spy the large brass key hanging from a wooden peg driven into a post nearby.

It almost would have felt like a trap, finding the key so easily. Calder slunk into the shadows, not retrieving the key until he was certain it wasn't a trap. That someone wasn't waiting for another to reach for the key.

Then again, why would they? And why would they want to keep the key hidden? There was no reason for stomach, heavy with another baby, was taxing her every move.

She admired the way Calder held his son, the handsome figure he made. Not a single day had she regretted the choice she'd made to make a life with him.

They'd found an isolated region full of wildlife and plants as food sources with easy access to water, and a hill to build a cabin on. A cabin protected by the mountain behind them.

They'd been there a few months when Brenna had discovered they were not far from her father's lands. She'd told Calder.

He'd asked her if she wanted to visit her father, his jaw tight. She knew it wasn't her father that concerned him—it was the husband she'd left behind. As far as she was concerned, that man had not been her husband. They'd never consummated their marriage as man and wife. She'd never been much more than chattel to her husband, or even her father.

No, Brenna had told him. She had no wish to see anyone from her prior life.

Calder had nodded and acquiesced, though she knew his Viking blood wanted to seek revenge on the man who'd caused her such pain. For Brenna, there had been no reason for that.

She wanted peace and happiness. And listening to the sounds of Gunnar's merriment, feeling the baby she'd made toward his brother was the image that she carried on her mind as sleep overtook her.

That, and Halvar's words whispered to Calder.

"Brother, help me."

But this time, his brother wasn't laying near the fire.

"Halvar?" Calder kept his voice low so as not to disturb his family.

Maybe his brother had stepped away to relieve himself.

Calder paced the fire to wait, paced because something had left him—and his bear—unsettled.

He inhaled and tried to pick up other scents with his sensitive shifter senses. He blocked out the fire's aroma and sought something... anything.

Blood!

But whose—

That was when he heard it. The tiniest of sounds.

He glanced about him, trying to place the noise, to locate the source. Calder stepped away from the fire and began to survey the perimeter of their camp.

There!

He ran toward Halvar.

His brother was leaning against a tree, blood flowing from a slash in his throat.

"Brother!" Calder reached to hold up the slowly falling Halvar, sliding down the tree's rough bark.

Placing his hands under his brother's arms, he kept him from dropping to the ground.

"What—" Calder noticed the bloody blade in Halvar's hand. "No, Halvar. No!"

"I cannot live this way." And with that, Halvar's eyes closed, and his heart stopped beating.

At the same moment, Calder's bear fell silent again, his presence once more gone.

"Calder?"

Brenna stood not far, silhouetted by the fire.

Calder adjusted his body, so she couldn't see the horror.

"Go inside. I'll be there in a little." He fought to keep his voice from choking, to keep her from knowing.

She should not have to bear this burden as well.

"I'll be waiting."

"Sleep," he told her. "I may be a while."

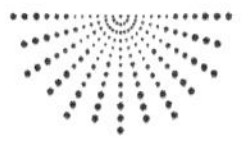

CHAPTER TWENTY-ONE

It was near dawn when Calder joined Brenna in the bed.

"Halvar?" Was her only whispered word.

"Yes."

A single tear made its way down her face. For this, he was thankful. This woman of his, she'd forgiven his brother and he'd had peace for a few days, enjoying his nephews, laughing once more.

Calder sent a word of thanks to his own bear for not turning on him this way. And it was then that Calder swore to himself that he would not let Halvar's death go unavenged.

He might not personally seek vengeance himself, as that would break Brenna's heart, but Calder would make sure his sons knew of this tragedy. Of the stories of the

Valkyrie and how they'd been created and the way their witch had destroyed his tribe and their bears. And Halvar. And Calder's bear.

A fury burned in Calder, and if he did not have his woman and children to consider, he'd have sought revenge.

Brenna's eyes were on his face, and he wondered how much of his emotions he'd allowed to show.

"I wonder if your bear would do that to you."

He took her face in her hands, gently, pulling her lips close to his. "Never."

"How can you know?"

"I do. I simply do." He studied her face. "I need to send Halvar off properly."

She waited, letting him speak his piece.

"I have to take him to the ocean. Build him a raft. Set him to sea in a pyre."

"I am not familiar with your ways…"

"It is not something I need help with," he assured her.

"But I will not let you go alone. Gunnar and Torsten and I will go with you."

He shook his head. "No, it's not right to make you three go out in the cold."

She took his face in her hands, mirroring what he had done, only her grip was much fierce. "I will not take no for an answer. I must be with you. Must make sure your bear is true to you. That he does not betray you as Halvar's betrayed him."

Calder knew there was no way to argue with this woman. He could tell her mind was set. "We shall leave tomorrow morning, then."

"The children and I will be ready to go."

He kissed her lips. "You do not need to. I assure you." Still hoping to change her mind.

"I know." Her expression turned serious, pensive. "We will not be far from the village, true?"

She didn't have to say what village. The village of the damned incident where he lost his men and his bear.

"True."

"I would like to leave the children with you and go talk to Freyja."

He contained a snarl. The witch that caused all this.

"Why would you want to do that?" He wondered if he really needed to ask that question, but he needed to be sure.

"To beg her to return your bear. To find a way not to let what happened to Halvar happen to you."

He exhaled in frustration. Why didn't she believe that his bear—his relationship with his bear—was different than Halvar's situation.

She took his hand in hers. "Please."

He studied their hands, hers so small next to his own. How could this woman, smaller than he, less powerful than he, hope to protect him? He realized this was important to her. How could he deny her? And then a thought occurred to him.

"What if they decide you're the enemy, since you now consort with the enemy?"

"Do you not trust me to speak carefully?"

He let the matter drop.

CHAPTER TWENTY-TWO

Brenna walked toward the village slowly, reflecting on the day's events.

After a beautiful ceremony, attended by the tiny family of four, Calder had set the torch to the raft with Halvar's body and set his brother adrift to return to whatever gods their people prayed to. She'd left their sons with Calder in the cave where they'd once sought refuge, and made her way to the village.

Nearing the village, Brenna picked up the scent of smoke from the fires, of cooking, of enjoyment. She heard the voices of merriment and happiness. She also picked up the sounds of weapons clashing, metal clanging, the grunting of effort during battle.

What was this?

Why did she hear the noise of battle coupled with the laughter of delight?

She stepped into the clearing and found herself faced with a spectacle she could not have imagined.

Eerika and Astrid, dressed in armor, bearing shields and axes, swords as well, were sparring.

Surrounding the two were an assortment of women, also attired the same way, also sporting weapons of war.

Brenna froze. She studied the visage before her.

What was missing?

Men.

There were no men.

Then she noticed the sounds had stopped, and all the women had turned to look at her.

"Brenna?" Astrid strode toward her followed by Eerika.

"Is it really you?" Eerika frowned. "Can it be?"

"It is I." Brenna didn't step forward, still caught off guard by the spectacle. "What are you doing?"

"Training," Eerika proclaimed, striking her shield with her sword proudly.

"Training for what?" Brenna frowned. "Where are the men?" Surely the village had some men? It had been several years. Had they not found new husbands? Had other family members not joined the women? "Won't they protect you?"

"Men?" a woman behind Astrid scoffed. "My mother has made men obsolete and unnecessary to our world."

Brenna looked hard at the woman. "Helga?"

"Indeed. Proud daughter of Freyja." The woman then mimicked Eerika's motion and struck her shield with her axe.

Freyja! The very woman who could help Brenna. "Where is your mother now?"

"She is not here." Helga's eyes narrowed. "Why do you ask?"

"I seek her assistance."

Astrid and Eerika stepped forward, pulling Brenna away and out of earshot of the group. Helga followed, staying slightly away, but still close enough to hear.

"What happened to the man you forsook us for?" Eerika hissed.

"Where is he? Did he perish?" Astrid's expression was hopeful.

Brenna quickly realized there would be no help and no quarter given by these women. There would be no help for Calder. She had to extricate herself as swiftly as she could, without giving away that Calder was well and alive.

"I traveled here alone, did I not?" She raised a brow and locked gazes with Astrid, who seemed to be the leader, though Eerika could be a close second.

"What is your business with my mother," Helga insisted.

"I was hoping for her expertise. Perhaps some training in her skills."

Eerika folded her arms over her chest. "Why is it that your father and husband say they have not seen you? Astrid saw your father. He declared you dead. As did your husband."

Brenna swallowed uncomfortably. "I am dead to them. How did Freyja make them obsolete? What about having children?"

Astrid and Eerika belted out bawdy laughter, looked at each other as though enjoying an inside joke.

"We find ones that can serve that purpose," Astrid informed her.

"And the only babies we give birth to are girls." Helga's tone carried pride.

"If you're traveling alone, and have no home, join us." Astrid picked up a sword and shield from a pile of weapons and held them out to Brenna.

Brenna thought of her two sons. She had questions, but more than anything, she was anxious to be gone from this place.

The bitterness the women harbored was evident and understandable, but Brenna did not share in the sentiment. She had a good man, two wonderful sons, and a third child on the way. She had no desire to be a part of a group that so clearly had no use for men.

"I cannot. I must be on my way. I had hoped that I would see Freyja, but since she is not here..."

"My mother does not stay in any one village. She visits several. She is worshipped among our people, viewed as much more than a high witch. She's godly born and divine fated."

"Thank you, sisters." With this final word, Brenna made her way from the village that so much history had been made.

She had her own history to make.

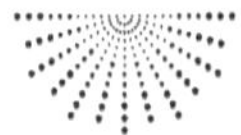

CALDER'S FIGHTING SONS

Years later.

Calder studied his sons. All three, now nearly men. Gunnar, Torsten, and Halvar. The last, born not long after his brother Halvar's death.

Gunnar pulled back the string on the bow and nocked the arrow.

Careful, son, do not let the elk hear you.

But Calder did not voice the thought. He'd brought his boys up well, they were strong hunters, good men. He and Brenna had done a fine job. He cast a glance backward at the woman who'd claimed his heart.

She caught his gaze and smiled back. She'd never told him what resulted from her visit to the village all those years ago, the visit that he knew she'd hoped would set his bear free. That had never happened.

What did happen, which was the final stroke that led Calder to tell his sons about his life's dream—he'd learned his sons had bears. And like his bear, theirs were chained to never make their presence known.

He'd learned this when Gunnar was six summers old. Gunnar had come to him, told him he could hear a roaring, but could not find the animal that caused the roar anywhere in the forest.

That was the day that broke Calder's heart. His son's bear was a prisoner. It was the curse that he carried and passed on to his sons.

He'd found out, as the years progressed, that the curse passed on to each of his sons.

His hatred had grown renewed for the witch Freyja who had not only killed his men and taken his bear, but also killed his sons' animals.

The last part of the curse, well, Calder had not learned that immediately.

Oh, no. That had been revealed to him two years ago when he and his family had been set upon by vagabonds who traveled through the wilderness and made victims of all they came across.

It was when this group made the fatal mistake to attack Calder and Brenna's family that Calder learned the nature of the final part of the curse that Freyja had visited upon them.

Oh, yes, this curse that caused him and his sons to become like beasts in battle, cutting down the men, moving with a speed and a bloodlust with vastly more ferocity than any shifter Calder had ever known.

The curse's overpowering strength was such that Calder caught Torsten's hands around Brenna's neck when he pulled him off her.

The bloodlust blinded Torsten to all but the others who would berserk, killing at will.

Torsten had shed tears, putting his young head in his mother's lap and begging her forgiveness.

And Calder's fury and hatred for Freyja and her kind burned more fiercely than he could have thought possible. It was because of her he lost his bear, and nearly lost his mate.

After the melee, after the brigands that had set upon Calder's family were dead, Calder took his sons out to the forest to talk to them, to explain what had happen.

He'd told them about the village. Their people. How they had once been bear shifters and now were cursed by the witch. How his boys carried the curse, and as far as he could tell, it would be transferred as such, from father to son.

He also told them about the Valkyrie, a secret he hadn't even told Brenna about.

For Calder held a secret. On his many hunting trips, he'd not only brought back meat to sustain his family, he'd visited the village where it all began.

He'd seen the women. The Valkyrie. He'd noted the way they trained. He'd witnessed their hatred of men.

And he'd fostered his own hatred. He'd noted the Valkyrie. He'd seen an occasional visit from Freyja. And he would have attacked, if he'd thought for a moment he could be victorious. The thought that he might lose his life and leave his mate to fend for herself and their sons had stayed his hand and his temper.

It had not, however, quenched his thirst for vengeance. He would carry this desire, and he would pass it on to his sons, that was his intent.

So, he'd told his sons about the witch and the Valkyrie, their uncle Halvar. He'd told them everything, and when they grew older, he'd taken them to see the Valkyrie village. He'd taken them three years in a row, until the last time, when they'd found the village gone, all signs of where they'd gone carefully hidden.

Calder and his sons had scouted, studied the ground for any sign of which direction the women had gone. There was no hint, no clue. It was obvious there was a deliberate attempt to keep their tracks hidden.

Why? Did they know he was watching them? Did they know he targeted them? Spied on them? Was that why they'd moved?

"Where do you think they went?" Gunnar had asked him.

"I do not know, son." But he made it his mission to find out.

And his sons had made it their missions as well. And their sons' sons. And so on, and so forth, through the generations, the rivalry of the Valkyrie and the berserkers was born and fostered.

There would be no peace between them until the berserkers' bears were returned to them.

SECOND EPILOGUE

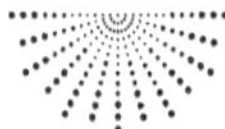

FREYJA'S FINAL WORDS

In a village far from the cave, far from the massacre that had happened so many years ago, Brenna visited a merchant.

No longer was she recognized, no longer did she fear being discovered by her father or the abusive husband she'd once had.

Still, she covered her hair, wore a scarf so it would hide part of her face, because, ultimately, she did wonder if she'd be found out. If Calder would be discovered. If the Valkyrie would wreak havoc on her life.

She ran the fabric the merchant carried between her fingertips, knowing his was not something she'd be able to afford. She'd chosen her life, and she did not regret it. Fabrics from far away were not to be a part of it.

A wonderful mate and three healthy sons were the path she'd taken.

She had no qualms regarding the choices she'd made.

"You have fine sons," a voice said.

Brenna knew that voice, but had not heard it in years and years. She turned slowly to face the speaker.

She stared at the woman. She knew her.

Freyja.

That Freyja knew of her family was a frightful thought. This witch was not to be trifled with. Brenna remained calm, no small task. She looked around to be sure they had no witnesses or eavesdroppers. "You know I have more than one?"

Freyja nodded. "I do. And like their father, they cannot shift."

Brenna lowered the fabric, stepped closer to Freyja to keep their conversation even more private. "Because of you."

Freyja's smile was tight. "Because of the action they took against our own people. The atrocities."

Brenna acknowledged with a nod. It was not untrue; the clansmen of Calder had not been good to Freyja's village. "So, you know of my sons, and my mate."

Freyja inclined her head. "I do."

"And yet you've not sought to harm them. Us."

"You spared my niece."

Brenna cocked her head, studying the almost-unaging witch. "Eerika?"

Freyja rewarded her with a slight smile. "My youngest sister's firstborn."

"She saved me once, long ago," Brenna added, and then the thought occurred to her. A thought that made her flesh crawl and her blood run through her body with the burn of ice water. "And now? Will you seek to exact revenge on my sons?"

Freyja shook her head. "I shall not, but their kind will always do battle with the women of my daughter's descendants. They'll be locked in an eternal struggle that can only be solved in one of two ways. The eradication of either breed, which would end all the battling, or if the berserkers learn how to turn their kind back into shifters."

"You could put an end to this, Freyja. It is in your power."

"It no longer is."

"How can that be?"

"My daughter Helga and Eerika are no longer alive. Killed in battle. Astrid has moved the Valkyrie into hiding."

"You are a powerful witch. You can find them if you wish. You can change the course of this."

"Oh, but I cannot change the course. I cannot reverse my spell. And I cannot find the Valkyrie. They have located a council of witches whose joint power exceeds my own. Their spell keeps my seekers from finding the

Valkyrie. And now that Helga is no longer with them, I have no blood connection to use to see."

Brenna exhaled. "And so, it is to be like this? Forever more?"

Freyja shrugged. "There are ways to change the course, but those are not for me to speak."

Brenna entered the cabin and dropped the bag of sundries she'd acquired at the traveling merchant's.

No Calder. No sons.

She stepped outside just in time to see them entering the clearing.

Four fine figures of men. She filled with pride at the sight of them, thankful they were hale and hearty.

Her gaze centered on Calder, who still made her heart beat faster and her body course with a heat she'd never lost.

His gaze locked with hers.

He pointed to Torsten and Halvar. "The boys have done some fine hunting."

She smiled at her sons. "I see it was a good trip for you."

"And yours?" he asked.

She'd keep her secret, she decided. "It was a good trip as well. The merchant had much to choose from."

He stepped closer, kissing her lips, the amber flame of his bear flickered in the depths of his eyes.

She savored the taste of his lips, wrapped her arms around his neck.

"I am happy you are home," she whispered. "Finally."

"Always."

KEEP READING FOR AN EXCERPT FROM THE NEXT BOOK IN the series!

CHALLENGE

Range and his small but lethal pack of dire wolves have been the go-to guys for Mae Forester.

But Mae didn't send them this gig. It came out of the blue.

Range and his team not in a position to turn down a buck, not these days.

The picture of a violet-eyed beauty in the assignment file further complicates matters.

Visit www.ElleThorne.com to sign up for Elle's newsletter!

CHAPTER 1

Isolated Region, Alaska.

R ange dropped his gear at the back door.

"How's the hunting," Asa asked.

"Got one waiting to be dressed." Deer. Range loved his venison.

"Dressed? Do you really plan to cook it?"

Range shrugged. Normally, he and his three brothers would simply shift into their wolves and feed on the carcass. "Davin griped last time that we don't act civilized often enough."

Asa laughed. "So, you're going to humor him and cook?"

"Hell, no," Range laughed with his brother, "He's doing the cooking. And he's dressing the deer." He put his rifle on the rack in the utility room.

"Shit, that reminds me, a call came in on the business line."

The business line. The line they used for the contract work they picked up.

"Mae called?" he asked.

"No," Asa looked puzzled, "some dude. Name was George something or another. Said he had a job for us."

"Hmmm. Wonder who gave him our number?" It wasn't that Range and his three brothers didn't freelance for people other than Mae Forester of Bear Canyon Valley, it was just that Mae was the one who usually put them in touch with those that needed them.

Mae Forester had been a part of Range and his brothers' lives since they were little tykes. Mae, who'd seen them fed and raised without being killed. Mae who'd kissed their cheeks and bid them farewell when they'd joined the Shifter Special Forces, SSF.

And finally, Mae who'd advised them not to join a research program that one of the commanders of Shifter Special Forces had offered them.

They'd joined the program. For a whole year, they'd agreed to be guinea pigs. Poked, prodded, stuck with needles, monitored, and tested.

They said that Range, Asa, Davin, and Jason would be stronger and perform better.

They never mentioned there might be complications. Fuckers.

The four brothers had left the program early,

finished their time with the SSF, and left all that behind, taking with them only the medals they'd earned for heroic acts and the complications that had come from the testing.

Complications that every now and then, would rear their ugly heads and mess up their lives.

Range had taken the money they'd all pooled together and bought property in Alaska, some mighty remote property where they didn't have to deal with people. Or other shifters, or anyone.

Occasionally, Mae would reach out and give them a job. Something that kept their bank account from hitting rock bottom. She'd told them with their skills, they could put themselves on the market and make a lot more.

But money hadn't been something they needed. Not much.

Until now.

One of their former team members in the SSF had called. His daughter had a disease that Range couldn't even dream of pronouncing. The treatments were ridiculously expensive, and wouldn't you know it, they weren't covered by the SSF insurance plans.

Range had to tell Vince that he couldn't help him, but he'd ask around. That had been yesterday. Then he'd tried to reach Mae at her hair salon, Forester Cuts, but had to leave a message for her to call him.

Now it looked like she'd drummed up some business, so maybe they could help Vince out.

"Got a number for this George guy?"

"It's on the pad by the phone."

Range kicked his boots off and pulled a lager out of the fridge.

Jason happened to walk in and see his older brother getting the beer out. "I don't know why you bother."

It wasn't a secret that shifters didn't get inebriated from alcoholic beverages.

"I like the taste," Range grumbled. "I don't need a nagging wife." He delivered a mock punch to Jason's shoulder.

Jason pivoted and dropped, then popped one toward Range's jaw.

Range drew back. His shifter speed was supernatural, but after all the testing, he was even faster than most shifters.

Jason laughed. "I miss it."

Range knew what he meant. He missed the military life. The missions. The occasional gig these days didn't do much toward recreating the action they used to have on an almost-daily basis.

"Me, too." Range downed half the bottle in one swig. "I've got a phone call to make. Hopefully there's a job for us that will let us help Vince."

"Hopefully," Asa added.

RANGE PUT THE PHONE DOWN, A STUNNED LOOK ON HIS face. When things seemed too good to be true, they usually were. He dialed Mae's number.

The other end was answered on the first ring. "Forester Cuts." Mae's voice.

"Mae."

"Range!" Mae sounded happy to hear from him.

As always, her voice made him feel like he was in a different time, a different place.

"I just got your message. Doc and I were on the mountain, sorry."

"No problem. How's Doc?"

"He's great." Mae's voice had a smile in it. "What's going on?"

"Well, I originally called to see if you might have a job—we could use a little money." He didn't want to tell her why. He wasn't sure if Vince would appreciate it. "But I'm guessing you know that since we already got a call. You sent George our way?"

There was a pause on the other end of the line, then, "No. I didn't recommend you to anyone recently. I usually don't give anyone direct access to you guys."

"Odd," Range muttered.

"But you do have a reputation for getting things done. I'm guessing word's gotten around, so it's not surprising you're getting calls."

Truth was, Range wasn't all that social, neither were

his brothers. If they'd had their druthers, they'd only deal with Mae.

The job had a nice price tag attached to it. And though he hadn't said yes, Range had told the man he'd be calling him back within the hour. He still had to discuss the details. He checked his email to see if the information that George had said he'd be sending had come through.

George. He seemed like a slick-talking character. Something about him rubbed Range the wrong way. Was it the nasally way he spoke or the autocratic tone in his voice? Either way, Range shoved those thoughts aside. His duty was to do the job, collect the cash, and help Vince.

"I'm sure you're right," he told Mae, his voice distracted.

"Are you okay, Range?"

He didn't want to tell her he was having aftereffects today, from the testing. He didn't want to worry her. She already felt bad enough for the choice he'd made to be a part of the testing, even though he and his brothers were old enough to own their decisions when they'd made that one.

"I'm good, Mae. Just fine."

"Okay," Mae said, but it was clear from her tone that she doubted him.

He clicked refresh on the monitor. Yup. There was the email from George Skople.

"Hey, Mae, I'll give you a call later, all right?"

"Sure, Range. Give the guys a hug for me?"

He laughed. "I'll tell them you're sending hugs." Like he'd be hugging his brothers. He pressed the icon to end the call.

He opened the email and hit print without looking at the attached documents.

The first couple lines of the email said the client wanted an ex-girlfriend located. No need to bring her in, simply relay the address.

Hell, I can handle this one alone.

That way he could leave his brothers here in case another job came in.

Then he saw the price tag.

Finding an ex-girlfriend for $300,000?

Maybe she'd stolen a painting from the client's mansion or something.

He printed several copies, snatched them off the printer and took them to the kitchen where he heard his brothers carousing.

"Looks like we get to help Vince." He dropped the papers on the kitchen table. Four printouts, one laid in front of each chair at the table.

"I'll take this one alone, no need to trouble all of us."

"No, shit? I know Vince will be happy." Davin picked his copy up.

The others did the same.

Jason let out a wolf whistle. "Holy hell."

Range frowned and started to thumb through the copy he'd printed for himself.

He quickly saw the reason for Jason's whistle.

A stunning woman, tall, statuesque, a strong jawline, sexy lips, and eyes that looked like they burned with a deep violet fire.

"No wonder you want to take this job alone." Davin tapped him on the bicep with his fist. "I'll offer to do this, if you want to stay home."

Range ignored him, scanning the rest of the documents. "Why do you think he wants her so badly?"

Jason laughed. "Have you seen her?"

"I don't know," Range's wolf was sending out alarms.

Asa folded his arms over his chest. "I know. I know Vince's daughter needs the treatments. I know we don't look a gift horse in the mouth."

"Yeah," Range said, but still.

But still.

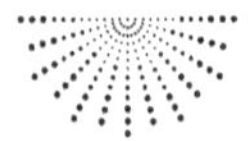

CHAPTER 2

The Heights, Houston, Texas. A week later.

E ira's phone rang.
Again.

For the millionth time, it seemed.

She rolled her eyes.

"Why did you give that guy your number?" Emme asked.

Eira didn't. She hadn't counted on the asshole taking her phone and using it to call himself. Stupid, stupid, stupid.Even more stupid that she hadn't replaced it yet. But a harmless one-night stand—what did it matter? She shook her head. "What is important now is that I need to not hear from him anymore." What a pain in the ass. One date, if you could call it a date, and now he had become a stalker. "I'm going to a couple places downtown tonight. On a case. Anyone want to join?"

"Places?" Hélène asked. "Care to be more specific?"

"Yes," Eira smirked, as if Hélène didn't know. "Couple of clubs."

"Oh! I'm in!" Lina beamed.

Her roommates never turned down a chance to go out.

"Who are we following?" Emme asked.

Eira ran a private investigation agency. Most of her cases revolved around cheating husbands and cheating wives. She made a hefty amount of money, courtesy of one of Houston's top divorce lawyers, who hired her for every case.

There were more difficult ways to make a living. Eira was more than sure of that, because she'd made a living in those other ways over the years.

Years?

More like centuries.

Eira was part of an ancient and immortal sisterhood. Not only was the sisterhood immortal, so were the members. And their kids.

Okay, well, there was one way—and one way only— they could die. But the sisterhood didn't age. They were frozen in their prime by the touch of the one who created them. Born mortals and turned to immortals in their twenties in a ceremony that was private and personal, and never discussed.

At the age of seven, all girls were sent to their training schools to learn the arts of their kind.

That art? Specifically, fighting. The sisterhood was composed of female warriors. Strictly. Men had no place in this sisterhood.

Once a year, each girl would be returned to her mother for a month before returning to the school to continue her education.

Where did men fit in? They didn't. Men's roles in the world of the sisterhood was simple. They had two purposes: procreation and the release of those needs that on occasion built up.

And so, it was with glee that several members of the sisterhood were looking forward to putting on their short skirts and heels and charming the pants off the mortal men while Eira was on assignment pursuing one dirt bag or another.

Eira was part of a group of four roommates, all in the sisterhood, of course. It wouldn't do to room with mortals. Too many questions would come up.

Their apartment was flanked by others from the sisterhood, four of them in the apartment on the left, and three in the apartment on the right.

The sisterhood lived together, based on sects. Sect members stayed near each other. They were not to reveal anything to others, humans or otherwise, else be put on trial by tribunal. A decision would be immediate. Sentence was carried out instantly.

These bad ass, hard ass women?

A proud and ancient breed, deciders of the slain.

And very capable of adding to the numbers of slain men over the millennia.

AFTERWORD

I hope you enjoyed *Origins!*
I can't wait for you to read the next story!

Another hot wolf shifter. Another sassy, bootylicious woman. Another sexy story!

Check out www.ellethorne.com for more of the Shifters Forever Worlds! There are more than forty shifter stories with their wonderful happily ever afters! And wait until you meet the witches of New Orleans, and the elementals of Colorado, not to mention the polar bears of New

York and Russia. So many shifters! So many love stories! Enjoy!

SHIFTERS FOREVER SERIES

Are you ready for it?

I have a whole world full of shifters to share with you.

I'm listing them here, in the suggested reading order, though I've tried to make it so that you can pick up anywhere in the series as we all have probably done that at one point or another.

Many of these are organized in box sets for savings. Be sure to visit www.ellethorne.com to see which box sets are out!

Where's the best place to start? Well, probably with SHIFTERS FOREVER.

SHIFTERS FOREVER

Grizzly bear shifters and their mates steam up the pages in these swoon-worthy paranormal romances. From trespassers with hidden agendas to curvaceous women who are ready to take a chance, the stories in this collection will capture your heart.

- PROTECTION
- SEDUCTION
- PERSUASION
- INVITATION
- TEMPTATION
- ATTRACTION

ALWAYS AFTER DARK

A spinoff with the white tiger from Shifters Forever: Vax, born Vittorio Tiero. He's the one that helped Kane out during a shifter battle. Follow the Tiero family, a group of white tiger shifters, as they head to America to find love… and heart-stopping danger. Full of romance, suspense, and gritty drama, this red-hot collection is sure to entertain!

- CONTROVERSY
- TERRITORY
- ADVERSARY
- SANCTUARY

NEVER AFTER DARK

Another spinoff that takes place in Europe. Here we visit cities along the Mediterranean and meet the old school Tiero white tiger shifters who are resistant to change.

- FORBIDDEN
- FORSAKEN
- FORGOTTEN
- FOREPLAY

ONLY AFTER DARK

Taking place in New Orleans, the Arceneaux shifters, led by Lézare, Vax's white tiger cousin—on his mother's side—are sure to capture your hearts. The Arceneaux are the black sheep of the family. Lézare doesn't cave to public opinion. He dictates policy in the area he rules and he shuns old school European rules and regimes.

- DESIRABLE
- INSATIABLE
- COMBUSTIBLE
- UNDENIABLE
- INEVITABLE
- INESCAPABLE

BITTER FALLS FOREVER

This romance features Mae Forester's nephew Dane Forester, a freewheeling, sexy, successful, movie star who uses every role and every woman to escape and forget the heartbreak he left in Bitter Falls.

- UNBOUND

BARELY AFTER DARK

This series features more of Mae Forester's nephews! Grizzly bear shifters steam up the pages in these swoon-worthy paranormal romances. From trespassers with hidden agendas to curvaceous women who are ready to take a chance, the stories in this collection will capture your heart.

- CROSS
- LANCE
- JUDGE

EVER AFTER DARK

Get ready to be introduced to the white tigers you learned to love in Always After Dark, Never After Dark, and Only After Dark. See their heritage. Visit Giovanni Tiero and his brothers Federico and Tito. Get reacquainted with Isabel Tiero and meet her sister Capriana

Valenti.

- STONEBOUND
- FORMIDABLE

SHIFTERS FOREVER AFTER

This series follows a group of polar bears in New York. Russian and rumored to be mobbed up, they are a powerhouse of shifters, determining the fate of many on the East Coast. Mikhail Romanoff, Layla's father, runs this outfit with an iron fist. Layla's sexy cousin Malachi features prominently in this series.

- COMPLICATION
- FASCINATION
- MOTIVATION
- CAPTIVATION
- FLIRTATION
- INFATUATION

FOREVER AFTER DARK

A series which takes place in Denver, Colorado. Enter a world of secrets and forbidden love. Panther shifters who who share their worlds with elementals must decide who they can trust—and who they can't live without.

- NOTORIOUS

- SCANDALOUS
- DELICIOUS
- PERILOUS

SHIFTERS FOREVER MORE Grizzly bear shifters, dragon shifters, sorceresses, elementals, and all types of other paranormal beings and their mates steam up the pages as the Bear Canyon Valley clan sorts through trespassers with hidden agenda, hidden military compounds, top secret experiments and curvaceous women who are ready to take a chance. The romances in this collection will capture your heart and leave your head spinning!

- CONFUSION
- DECISION
- POSSESSION
- ILLUSION
- PASSION
- IMPRESSION

FINALLY AFTER DARK
Follow a pack of dire wolves as they encounter Valkyrie

and Berserkers and determine the origins of their kind throughout the ages, while discovering their fated mates.

- ORIGINS
- CHALLENGE
- DAMAGE
- RAVAGE
- MORE TO FOLLOW!

I do hope you'll be able to join me on this wonderful journey with our Shifters Forever Worlds Shifters and their mates!

To receive exclusive updates from Elle Thorne and to be the first to get your hands on the next release, please sign up for her mailing list.

Elle Thorne Newsletter

If you can't click, just put this in your browser:
http://www.ellethorne.com/contact

MY PERSONAL GUARANTEE:

THIS WILL ONLY BE USED TO ANNOUNCE NEW RELEASES AND SPECIALS. AND TO GIVE MY WONDERFUL SPECIAL READERS A LITTLE GIFT.

SHIFTERS REALMS

I have another new world of shifters! How exciting! I can't wait to share them with you!

Be sure to visit www.ellethorne.com to see which ones are out!

Where's the best place to start? Here we go!

IRON FLATS

Wolf shifters and their mates steam up the pages in these paranormal romances. From rovers with hidden agendas

to women who are ready to take a chance, to unknown
the stories in this collection will capture your heart.

- IRON FLATS EXILE
- IRON FLATS JUSTICE
- IRON FLATS REBEL
- IRON FLATS MAVERICK

MORE TO FOLLOW!

*I do hope you'll be able to join me on this wonderful journey
with our Shifters Forever Worlds Shifters and their mates!*

To receive exclusive updates from Elle Thorne and to be
the first to get your hands on the next release, please sign
up for her mailing list.

Elle Thorne Newsletter

If you can't click, just put this in your browser:
http://www.ellethorne.com/contact

MY PERSONAL GUARANTEE:
THIS WILL ONLY BE USED TO ANNOUNCE NEW RELEASES AND
SPECIALS. AND TO GIVE MY WONDERFUL SPECIAL READERS A
LITTLE GIFT.

Shifters Forever Worlds

Shifter Realms

For sales and news, sign up for the newsletter! Thank you for purchasing and downloading my book. Words can't express what it means to me. If you enjoyed this read, please remember to take a second to leave a review. I'd love to know what your favorite parts were.

The fun isn't about to stop. Make sure you sign up for the link to the newsletter.

Hearing from you means the world to me. This would not be possible without you and your love for reading.

With much gratitude, I thank you!

It took Elle Thorne years to stop being a closet romantic.

Originally from Europe, she wouldn't dream of living anywhere else but Texas. Unless it was another southern —translation: warm!—state. A southern European by birth, she wants to be near the water and the Mediterranean temperatures if possible.

Where does she like to hang out? Near a lake, a beach, preferably with a latte—extra shot of espresso, please! She's inspired by the everyday men who make dreams come true. She loves a roughneck, especially one with a callous or two on his hands. A man who knows how to fix a car, please a woman, and protect what's his.

Nothing less will do.

ELLE'S NEWSLETTER

To receive exclusive updates from Elle Thorne and to be the first to get your hands on the next release, please sign up for her mailing list.

Put this in your browser:

www.ellethorne.com/contact

My personal guarantee:

This will only be used to announce new releases and specials. And to give my wonderful special readers a little gift.